I0574396

ISBN 979-8-9925366-1-4

"Ramps and Rocket" copyright 2019 by Alicia K. Anderson. First appeared in *Grimm, Grit, and Gasoline* (World Weaver Press: Albuquerque)

"Special Interest" copyright 2021 by Alicia K. Anderson. First appeared in *Dark cheer: Cryptids Emerging, Volume Blue* (Improbable Press: Victoria, Australia)

"Vivien's Heir" copyright 2023 by Alicia K. Anderson. First appeared in *Mirrors Reflecting Shadows* (Anxiety Press / Outcast Press / Row Faineant Press)

The story, all names, characters, and incidents portrayed in this production are fictitious. No identification with actual persons (living or deceased), places, buildings, and products is intended or should be inferred.

Cover Art by Katherine Lynn Bierman
https://katherinelynnbierman.com/

MAGIC, MURDER, AND MACHINES

REIMAGINING FAIRY TALES

ALICIA K. ANDERSON

ALICIA KING ANDERSON, PH.D.

ACKNOWLEDGMENTS

For Josh,
who shows me every day
what it means to be believed in

This book would not be possible without the support of the Morbid Anatomy community and my patrons.

Special thanks to Kt, Ame, John, Lex, Renée, Alicia, Gilena, Victoria, Christine, and Vince.

1

MACHINE LEARNING

Nervous muttering flickered beneath the hum of the old fluorescent light bars swaying from the ceiling. I could hear the crunch of broken glass grinding to powder under the soles of my boots. Eyes followed me without following me. If they were not looking at me directly, that didn't mean they weren't paying attention.

I reached the frosted glass window of the only door in the warehouse. It swung open before I could knock. Like the downcast eyes of the others in the sofas and workstations behind me, they were watching, too.

The Goon opened the door without a word. The Boss nodded, and Goon stepped aside allowing me to enter. Goon shut the door soundlessly behind him, his own feet somehow making no sound on the debris on the floor.

"Send me." I said to the Boss.

"Shar, don't be an idiot." The Boss's eyes flickered black and mean in the light of the little green accountant's lamp on his desk. He pressed his palms flat on the sleek mahogany.

"He killed Mariam. Send me." I had nothing left to live for without her.

"What about Dunya?" Funny that he thought my little sister was something to live for, when he had taken her away years ago. She was his bargaining chip. Her welfare in exchange for my work.

"She'll be fine. You'll take care of her." I took a step toward the desk. "I want to go, Boss. I can do it. I can stop him."

"When Mariam couldn't?" The air sucked from my chest at the verbal jab. She was the best of us. The best of what was left of me. I didn't know I could succeed where she had failed. I didn't know anything except that I had to try. Maybe I could avenge her. Maybe I could redeem myself.

The Boss drummed his fingers on the desktop, staring at me while he thought. His jaw worked back and forth with effort. "You look like shit. Go home. Get cleaned up. Put your affairs in order." His fingers stopped moving. "You'll go tomorrow morning."

I blinked, then nodded. Grateful and terrified at the same time, I swallowed my smartass remark and left the office.

I was next.

I SHARED a room in a condemned hotel run by some neo-woolies. The western half of the building had been shirred off in a blast a few years ago. It wasn't structurally sound, or legal, but it was home for me and a few hundred others.

"You're home early." Layla glanced up from the dick she was sucking when I opened the door.

"Is she joining us?" The john asked, smiling at me while he used his hand to urge Layla's head back toward his crotch.

"No." Layla and I said the word in unison.

She went back to fellating, and I grabbed my stuff and went to the bathroom for a shower. I stayed in the steaming cascade until I heard the door open and close, and the John make his way into the hall. *Put my affairs in order.*

I had on a flowing linen robe and a soft silk hijab by the time I went out to talk with Layla. She was poking at a suspicious dish of leftovers with a fork.

"What's the occasion?" she asked, motioning the fork at my getup.

"He killed Mariam yesterday." I curled up on the foot of my bed. "I'm going tomorrow."

Layla's skin turned a little green. With a squeak of styrofoam, she put the leftovers back in the mini fridge. She pulled out a bottle of beer and offered it to me.

"You know I don't drink."

"No time like the present."

"Even more important now."

With a shrug, she took a long pull from the beer and flopped onto her own bed. "What are you going to do?"

"What do you mean?"

"For your talent." She played with the bottle. "I thought about going and trying to blow him for mine. But Jez got killed when she tried that, and she was the best."

"I don't know. Code, I guess." I shrugged. "It's all I can do well."

"And you're going to marry him?" Layla raised her eyebrows.

"That's part of the whole deal, right?" I was embarrassed by the whole idea. Mariam had been my first – only – lover. I wasn't interested in men. Well, I wasn't interested in women, either. I was only interested in Mariam. And she was dead.

The adhan sounded in the hall. I could hear the head woolie's voice crackling "ʾAllāhu ʾakbar". Layla rolled her eyes at me as I grabbed my threadbare red rug and trotted down the hall to the rim of the obliterated edge of the building. All the others were setting up their rugs, facing West toward *qiblah*. As I repeated the words silently in my head, I inhaled the familiar scent of my little rug. I realized this may be one of my last moments of *salat*.

Allah listens. I know Allah listens. I prayed harder than I've ever prayed before. If I couldn't stop him, at least I'd save someone else from dying tomorrow.

Maybe that would be enough.

THE HOUSE the Goon took me to was like no place I'd ever seen. It was like a Hollywood movie oasis. Like something you'd imagine in old Dubai. Just inside the gates, a fountain splayed obscenely inside the circle that limousines were intended to maneuver. The fresh, clean water's splashing was almost offensive. I didn't care about the marble statues of naked women whose vaginas and breasts were the source of the fountain's arcs of water. The water was a ridiculous waste.

He wasted the lives of countless women, why would he care about water?

Nauseated, I stepped up the gleaming marble stairs. The Goon rang the bell. A servant of some sort opened the door. He eyed my hijab, tried to look through my dress to discern if I had a feminine body.

"She'll do." The servant motioned me inside and dismissed the Goon like he wasn't even standing there. My heart was hitting staccato rhythms in the back of my throat as I crossed the threshold that was very likely my last.

Just inside the door, there was a small *sebil* fountain in the antechamber like the house was some holy place and not a decadent hell made for women to die. I washed my hands, feet and face at it and followed the servant deeper into the house. I was carrying a small duffel bag. It held the laptop the Boss gave me and my prayer rug. I wouldn't need anything else.

The first thing I noticed were the cameras. The house was supposed to be discreet and posh, but there were cameras everywhere. There wasn't a dark angle. Some machines were monitoring millions of images and cataloging, compressing and compiling them. Indexing the interesting ones. There was no human mind that was managing that many cameras. It wasn't possible. It would take a staff of hundreds, and mostly they'd be bored out of their minds.

But I was a coder. That's what I did for the Boss. It's how I stayed alive. I could well imagine the program running those thousands of cameras. The Boss worked for this guy. It's entirely possible I wrote part of it.

The guy in question swept down a wide staircase. His warm brown fingertips traced the entire length of the glossy wooden handrail like a lover. He wore Eurofash like he was some 'Murican. The only way you'd know he was the same ethnicity as me was the deep brown of his eyes and the gentle brown of his skin.

"A faithful sister?" He grinned at my best green silk hijab. "How quaint!"

"Peace be upon you," I muttered the traditional greeting and lowered my eyes. Maybe if he thought I was docile, he'd get it over with quickly.

His teeth were too white. "The wedding ceremony is at three." He said the statement to the servant and to me. I got the impression the ceremony was *always* at three.

It was gross to notice that the baths had as many cameras as the foyer. Gross and not unexpected. Women had to try to escape, didn't they? The others? Before me? Or maybe some of them killed themselves. I imagined him watching the footage after he killed each one. Perhaps before. Maybe seeing how she faced her doom helped him decide what the manner of her death should be.

What he'd see of me was my body. Which he'd see after the wedding any way. And he'd see me praying on my little rug. When I had time, between combings and fittings and washings and shavings, he'd see me coding. I had an idea. I'd spend the night working on it. It was nearly done.

The ceremony was as tasteless and bile-raising as the fountain. A handful of faithfuls, including the Boss, and the servants who had to stomach yet another wedding surrounded the little altar in the back garden. I could see where dirt and weather and time had begun to wear at the crisp white coverings. The flowers were silk and starting to fray. The cameras gleamed in the afternoon sun like baleful eyes.

I swore I was his wife, and he, my husband. His teeth were still too white. Now he wore a traditional old-school medieval get-up. Like the kind from Fairy Tales. He had me dressed up the same way. Like we were going to grasp a carnelian talisman and ride away on a flying bed.

If I were so lucky.

The feast was subdued, and the "well-wishers" were about as excited as they'd be at a funeral. The Boss had the gall to wipe a tear away from his eyes. We huddled under a gossamer curtain while the women sewed love wishes into it and ground sweets together. I heard at least one prayer for my survival. We fed each other bites of honeycomb. He licked my fingers and I had to swallow a scream.

After the feast, he led me upstairs to the master suite, and I noticed there was finally a room without surveillance.

I didn't concentrate on his sweating and gyration on top of me. I was debugging the code in my mind. The code I had to finish immediately if it were going to save my life. The sex didn't hurt, but it didn't feel good, either. His skin was smooth and clammy. His penis was short and thick. I didn't care.

I requested my belongings to be brought to the master suite. It was my right, as the "lady of the house" now that we were married. The servants obliged. Then I answered the evening call to prayer on my little rug.

"I'd like to fuck you like that, Sharzâd. While you're praying. Your ass in the air."

I want to say that I was trying to hear and speak to Allah, and to remember that Allah loved me in that moment. But really, I was just glad my red face was facing the floor. He had taken off my hijab, and my short bob haircut barely covered the edges of my face where I tilted toward the West.

He came over to me then, wanting to get a rise out of me, while I prayed. I repeated the prayers in a whisper so not to lose track of where I was. He touched me while I prayed. I tried not to pay attention to it. I tried not to scream.

I kept praying.

Defiled. Embarrassed. I dragged my laptop onto the edge of the bed, and finished the code, praying the whole time I wrote it. He slept a little, then looked over my shoulder.

"Is this your amusement for me? Your skill?"

I closed the last missing bracket and compiled the code. It worked. "It is." The clock read 21:04. Perfect. I completed my prayer silently before I opened the GUI for the program I'd created.

"Please, Sharzâd. Before bed, please tell me a story."

My little sister Dunyazab's voice came from the laptop speakers. A little staticky and a little tinny, but still recognizable. It was a clip from a voice memo I'd saved just before the Boss had taken her away from me.

"May I tell you a story, sir?" I asked my husband. "Before we go to sleep?"

He lounged back against the pillows and smiled with his too-white teeth. "Why not? Go ahead."

I clicked the button. The program compiled from thousands of stories, thousands of tweets, reddit chains, memes, fairy tales, from folklore, and mythology. The screen displayed a story. Boxy green font on black screen.

2

RETRIEVING THE RIVER

"I used to catch big fish from this spot." The village soothsayer sat on a rock on the bank of what was once the river. He did not look at me as I approached him, my boots stirring up the dust. He looked north to the icy wasteland that had frozen our watersheds. "Big fish," he repeated.

His eyes were glassy and distant, like they got when the gods were talking to him. "You, Quiet Woman," he said, lifting a bony finger in my direction, "Go get my fish. Go get the water."

I wasn't sure how I was supposed to do such a thing. I had been approaching him to make sure he didn't fall down the crusty bank into the dry bed where the river should be. Shrugging, and saying nothing, I turned in the golden dust that used to be a lush riverbank. I wasn't expecting what would happen inside the keep.

Clatters of arms overhead rang through the courtyard. Stomping, armored feet battered the plank walkways and the walls.

"What's happening?" I asked. A goose girl flapped her arms at her charges to get them into the stable. She ignored me. "What's going on?" No one answered.

The guards in the towers were fighting one another. Each of the towers was clattering in turmoil. We needed them facing out, facing the four directions. Each of the four walls threatened us with its own kinds of danger. Yet, our protectors were fighting one another.

I climbed the first set of stairs, spiraling to the tower and the turrets on the eastern edge of the castle. It overlooked the riverbed I had just left. It watched the withered fields of brown grain stalks that needed the river to flourish. Beyond the fields were the Others' lands. The river used to protect our keep from them – or at least slow them down. No longer.

There were four guards in this tower. I heard them shouting above me as I wound my way to the top. My sword was loosened in its sheath. They could attack me as easily as they had one another.

They all spun, swords and pikes raised, to point them at me when I opened the door. I stayed in the threshold and moved slowly.

"Why are you arguing?" I asked them.

They spoke at once, and their voices combined. Staying quiet, I heard the real message under their words. "We are afraid." They each said it in different ways. Some used their wide eyes to tell me. Others used shouting, angry voices.

"What are you afraid of?" I asked them all, asking the question they prompted, though none of them had said those words.

They pointed their gazes and glinting swords at the tower to the south.

"Them."

"I will deal with them," I assured them. "Will you stop fighting one another and guard our people instead?"

"We will."

And they did.

I walked the plank walkways from the east to the south. The southern tower guarded against the forests and its deep unknowns. The forest had other rivers beyond ours, so it was still dense and green and full of bandits. The south tower guards were shouting at one another more loudly than the eastern ones had been. Just as before, I opened the door. Six weapons aimed at me in the south tower.

"Why are you arguing?" I asked them.

They spoke at once, and their voices blended. The message beneath their words was "We are angry."

"What are you angry about?" I asked them, though none of them had said those words.

They pointed their gazes and their weapons at the tower to the west.

"Them."

"I will deal with them," I assured them. "Will you stop fighting one another and guard our people instead?"

"We will."

And they did.

I walked along the planks from the south to the west. The western tower guarded the village and the shepherds with their flocks. The sheep had to walk farther to be plump this season, the brown scrub of grass was not close to the village and the keep. It was harder to protect them from the great wolves. The west tower guards were not shouting, but I heard a clash of arms behind the door. When I opened this door, they did not pause to acknowledge me.

"Why are you fighting?" I shouted over the crash of metal on metal and stone.

They did not speak, but I heard their answer, the message beneath their bruises and their bleeding. "We are sorrowful," they did not say.

"Why do you sorrow?" I asked them. I kept my voice quiet and low, as was my habit.

They stopped fighting. As one, the men of the western tower wept. One sat on the planks of the floor in his deep woe.

Without speaking, they motioned toward the tower to the north.

"I will go." I told them. "Will you stop fighting one another and guard our people instead?"

"We will."

And they did.

There was no plank walkway from any of the other guard towers to reach the tower to the north. I had to climb down the wooden ladders, and then spiral back up the stairs to reach the northern tower. As I climbed down hand over hand. As I climbed up step by step. I thought about the other towers. Fear. Rage. Sorrow. What misery awaited me in the tower of the north?

As I climbed, I noticed that an ivy vine had crept up this tower, and where the other walls were grey stone and clean and dry, this tower's walls were green with vegetation and dirt. Birds nested in the lofts and streaked the walls white. The tower smelled of earth and rot. The grey stone was pocked with decay. I climbed the spiral and heard nothing overhead.

There were no sounds coming from the tower room. There were no guards in the north tower. There never were. The north tower overlooks the vast expanse: the mountains, the snow fields and the lands of the Snow Queen and her dead. Nothing came from there. No one went there.

I opened the door – it took a shove to open it past the plants. When I opened the room, the only thing waiting for me, in a bed of flowers and ivy, was a chubby baby girl with curly black hair.

She gurgled at me as I lifted her.

I was not comfortable holding babies. They were fragile and soft, and I feared I'd break them. I held her far away from me, but she wriggled and squirmed. I held her close, and she grew still.

I walked her back down the spiral stairs and flowers followed us.

I reached the courtyard to explain to the citizens of our little town what I'd found.

"She is the source of the fear, the rage, and the sorrow," the people said. "We have to get rid of her."

"She is magic. Magic is dangerous."

The village soothsayer arrived. He led a great mammoth saddled for a hard journey. He handed its reins to me.

"The Snow Queen is expecting her," he said. "Go get the water, Quiet Woman."

No one from our town had ever been to the Snow Queen's fortress. We knew it was there – far to the north, gleaming with the lights. We knew she was the reason our river was dry. We had heard ancient stories about the way to reach her. But that's all I had to follow – stories. No map. No road. Vast frozen ice-crusted wastes of rock and snow. And stories.

The child was swaddled and tucked in a little basket. The basket was lined with mammoth wool and wrapped in oilcloth and leather. She was protected from the wind and what would be increasingly cold. I had similar layers of clothing and blankets for myself. I had bags that were packed by the soothsayer, containing whatever he thought I would need for this journey.

The mammoth snorted and burble-trumpeted to itself as it puffed its way north, enjoying the cooler temperatures and the rugged terrain of its ancestors. The baby girl and I settled in for our journey. No one knew how long it would take. As I left, I could hear the work men and their hammers repairing and cleaning out the northern tower. They would get it as fit and shining as the others. They would feed the plants to the livestock. Then, they would set a watch for my return.

If I returned.

Our first camp had no break from the howling wind or the hail that was ripped from the ledges and rained upon us. A spitting fire wouldn't take on the dried dung I tried to light. The mammoth hunkered, the baby and I hunkered against its side, huddled together through the night.

The mammoth taught us, or we all learned together, to travel through the colder nights, and sleep during the blinding days. The sun sparkling off the snow was no safer than the howling wind. And moving at night meant we have a better chance of living through the lowest temperatures.

The baby did not cry.

I had her huddled inside my clothes, skin to skin against my milk-less breasts. She rode against me, breathing hot baby breaths on my collarbone.

I had never wanted children. I became a warrior instead of a mother. But this baby. This baby was not a child. She was something else. I peeked down my shirt at her. Her black curls drifted against my skin. We held each other close on this journey.

The stories told of three huts and three women. Warm cookpots and food. Each helpful in her own way. Each could point to the next hut, or to the Snow Queen's castle. I found the first hut, and it was shattered. Empty. There was no woman. No warm cookpot. There was nothing left but the dried-wood bones of the hut where it once stood.

Was I on the right path? Was this mangled shelter a good sign – that the old stories had *once* been true? Or was this a harbinger of something worse to come?

We continued, huddled, and hunkered together in our silence. Why *was* this my journey to take? I wondered this as I felt the steady gait of the mammoth beneath me. My hips flowed with the mount, and my body drifted above it, aware only of the silent infant. The baby that did not cry. The soothsayer had been so sure I had to be the one to retrieve the river.

I was the one who went into the towers to see to the guards. I thought back to that decision. I knew I could do it. Get them to stop fighting. Maybe it's something to do with the way I hear things. The things people don't say.

Maybe that was why the baby was my job, too. She didn't cry. She didn't make many sounds, really, but I could hear when she needed a fresh cloth or something to eat. I knew when she was content. I knew when she was too warm or too cold. These weren't a mother's instincts. I didn't have those. But I could listen.

The second hut was covered in snow.

There was no smoke escaping from the tiny portal that still faced the sky. I clambered up to the hole and stuck my head in, then gagged on the smell of centuries-old fish and slightly fresher death.

The stories had once known there were three huts. Was it a good sign?

Did it matter?

The mammoth seemed to know what it was doing, and it had been a friendly shelter. I trusted its instincts when it took a sharp left around a jagged precipice of ice. There was no more day and no more night. There were the lights, bright and flickering against the sky, or there was the sun, blinding on the snow. It was both heaven and hell at once. I had never imagined anything like this place.

The smell of smoke reached my nostrils and I nearly shouted for it. The mammoth led us to a hut. A hut with a stream of steady smoke curling from the roof. It snorted and huffed in pride as I slid down, clutching the baby inside my shirt.

"Oh child! Get in here out of the cold!" An ancient face poked out the door. I could barely understand her since she had no teeth.

I hustled into the hut and found not one old woman, but three. The hides and fishes, pieces of the first two huts were cobbled and clabbered together, reinforcing this one. The cookpot on the fire bubbled with stew. I relaxed into the old stories.

The three women tutted over me. They tutted over the baby. They tutted over the mammoth outside, and one took grasses out to him from her mattress.

I handed them the most mysterious of the soothsayer's bags. They squealed with delight over dried fish skins covered in charcoal writing.

"We will save these for later." They smiled at each other and patted the skins. I was glad they liked the gift.

"I'm taking this baby to the Snow Queen." I said to them as they poured stew into bowls and mumbled together.

"Of course you are." The eldest one said. "No other reason to be up this far north."

"Is there anything…" I wanted to ask for help. I wanted to know what I was supposed to do.

"There is nothing we can give you that you don't already have." The soft, gnarled hand of the old woman patted mine. "You'll be fine."

"Be sure to visit us on your way back through." The youngest one said. I'm not sure how I know which was the eldest and which was the youngest. They all looked older than leather to me.

I ate. The baby silently barfed up the broth then fell asleep. I wrapped our bodies back up, bundled together, and headed back into the absence of night under blue and coral waves in the sky.

The Snow Queen's fortress was just ahead, they said. I did not know what their idea of just ahead was. But their presence comforted me. That they were there, in a hut, made me sure that no matter how far ahead just ahead was, I could get there.

The mammoth was still sucking the grass from its teeth when we saw the first tower.

The fortress truly was just ahead. It loomed and rose out of the ice as if it was ice or glass. It was white and gleaming. The flickering waves of light on the night sky were echoed on its smooth walls. It was terrifying and beautiful. The mammoth stopped at a gate which opened out onto a bridge. The bridge was too narrow for the beast to cross. I pulled a few bags from his back and dismounted. Then I turned his reins and sent him back to the hut with the three women. He wrapped his trunk around my head in an approximation of a hug and turned away.

The child and I were alone as I walked through the gate and across the slender bridge.

The wind was colder beyond the gate. The ice was slipperier. Everything was more terrible. The fortress looked like it was made of diamonds.

The baby girl had the hiccups against my ribcage. I didn't know why that calmed me, but it did.

There was no guard. There were no doors. There was only a wide series of archways that led me deeper and deeper inside the palace. As the winds receded, my footsteps echoed louder. As the cold receded, my breath sounded harsh in my own ears.

She was there. On her throne. Alone in a palace of ice. She had white-blond hair and white-blue eyes and white skin so pale you could see the blue of her veins beneath it. Her dress glistened, but I suspected it, too, may be made of ice. Or perhaps mirrors.

"I –" I coughed because I was not prepared to speak. Did I bow? Did I kneel?

"I brought you this baby." I tried again.

The Snow Queen jerked back as if I'd slapped her. "You brought me *what?*" The final consonant was percussive and crisp, like an icicle cracking.

I unwrapped my coats and my capes and my shirt and I drew the bundled baby away from my chest. She hiccupped in the cold air and blinked at the brightness of the room. My chest was frozen with her loss. The cold air on skin left moist by her breath was unbearable.

"The soothsayer said you were waiting for her. He said you would give us back our river." I was not eloquent. I did not have a speech prepared. I'd been so focused on the stories and the sheer weight of survival; I hadn't even bothered to think of what I would say when I reached the Snow Queen.

The Snow Queen rose from her crystalline throne and stepped down from her dais to get a closer look at the child. Her footsteps did not echo like mine did. Her breath did not rasp.

The child did not make a sound. But I knew she was confused and afraid. She did not cry. How would anyone else be able to take care of her?

"She won't cry," I told the Queen as the slender woman took the chubby life-filled bundle from my arms. "You have to learn her faces. Her ways of asking without asking."

The Snow Queen's eerie light eyes blazed as she looked at me and then at the child. "Hm," she said, "We'll see."

She bounced the baby in her arms. This creature of desolation and cold was more comfortable with the action of holding an infant than I ever could be, even after all this practice.

"You," she says, "will stay one night, here in my palace."

This startled me. I hadn't expected to stay after delivering the baby. It was not an invitation. It was a command.

"Yes, Majesty." Was Majesty the right term?

She flickered a hand, and a hallway opened beside us. She turned her back on me, her attention focused on the baby. Dismissed, I followed the new hall.

It ended in a small room. The room's walls were ice, but a thick mammoth skin lined the floor. A fire crackled in a slick, dripping hearth. A proper bed was pulled near the fire, covered with leathers and skins.

I sat on the edge of the bed, and I stared at my hands for a bit before I peeled off all my layers and layers of clothes. My chest still felt naked without the baby. I undressed down to my skivs and as I stretched out in the bed, the room seemed to grow dimmer. Less gleaming.

The first time I woke in the night, it was to the sound of the baby crying. My heart broke. I wailed with her in the night. Tears dripped from my nose and onto my bed. I heard her tiny throat calling out for something. I tried to wrench myself from my bed. To find her. To help her.

"Cry for me!" The Snow Queen shouted through the castle.

I could not move. I sobbed. I was like the baby. Crying and help-less. I could hear her fear, alone in the icy halls with the unforgiving queen.

"CRY FOR ME." The Snow Queen roared, and it felt like she was commanding *me* to cry, not the wailing infant. The baby cried even harder, and so did I. Helpless to rise and protect the child, I was trem-bling with rage. I was angry at the queen for abusing the baby this way. Angry at myself for bringing her to the palace. I pounded the mattress with my fist, filled with fury.

"KEEP CRYING!" The walls trembled. I felt so sorry. So sorry for the baby. I imagined her there, wailing alone in a world of dazzling ice. I wept for the child and for myself, stuck in this strange world alone.

Finally, the child cried herself to sleep. Or I did. Or both.

The second time I woke in the night, it was to the sounds of the baby laughing. I thought it was the baby. I had never heard her laugh before. I smiled at the ceiling in the darkness of my bed, and I started to giggle with her. I did not hear the Snow Queen laugh with us.

The third time I woke in the night, a black-haired girl stood in the threshold of my room. She had bare feet and wore a translucent green dress. She was slender, and perhaps on the cusp of womanhood. Even when it made no sense, I knew she was the baby that wouldn't cry. The baby I held to my chest the whole way to the Snow Queen's palace.

3

SUNRISE

At sunrise, the screen went dark.

"What? Where did the story go?" He sat up, frowning at the screen.

"I don't know. I guess I didn't debug it all the way." I had programmed it to shut down with the recorded moment of sunrise. "I'm sure I can fix it to figure out how it ends." I had programmed it to not start up until after sunset.

He frowned but rolled over and started to snore. Just a few hours later, the servants woke us up with a breakfast tray for two, the dishes rattling with their trembling hands. They were edgy and jumpy. He woke up and grabbed his coffee and a croissant before striding to the baths. "Fix it. I want to know the end of the story by nightfall."

"Yes, of course." I said. Did--

Did that mean I would be able to live another day?

I heard him mutter, "*She lives*," to the servants as he left the room.

I was bathed, clothed, pampered, and ignored. I didn't have to do anything to fix the program. It was already working exactly as intended. So, since I was expected to spend the day on my laptop anyway, I infiltrated the code for the camera network.

Taking breaks only to eat and pray, I recognized the system that was running the cameras. I realized I hadn't done the surveillance work, it had Mariam's signatures all over it. But I *had* done the guns. I hadn't noticed the guns hidden in plain sight everywhere until I realized that I'd coded them to respond to certain events, commands and camera signals. I remembered this job. It was when I'd met Mariam.

"*Dear Shar! Are you ready to finish the story?*" Dunya's voice said at sunset. Still blushing from my husband's touch, I clicked the button without asking him.

4

RIVER RETRIEVED

The third time I woke in the night, a black-haired girl stood on the threshold of my room. She had bare feet and wore a translucent green dress. She was slender, and perhaps on the cusp of womanhood. Even when it made no sense, I knew she was the baby that wouldn't cry. The baby I held to my chest the whole way to the Snow Queen's palace.

She didn't say anything. She just padded on bare feet to my bedside and held her arms open wide, like she wanted to be held. Hugged. I opened my arms to her, and she folded into me. She pressed her ear against my chest, listening for a long time to my heartbeat.

Like a spirit, she lost her body and entered mine. She was gone. She was me. I was her. We were.

A tear slipped from our eye as we added logs to the fire.

We walked back down the long corridor to the Snow Queen. She sat, lost in thought upon her throne.

"Have you seen the girl?" She asked us when she turned to see us there.

We nodded. We tried to smile. The Snow Queen slapped us

across the face, her hand leaving a cold, red print on our cheek. We cried out in pain, and tears flooded our eyes.

"Have you seen the girl?" she asked again.

"We are the girl," we said. "Or we were." She drew her hand back to strike us again, and we reacted together, the warrior and the child. We held her icy wrist in our warm hand. We laughed at her expression of chagrin.

"You don't need me anymore," the Snow Queen wrenched her hand away from our grasp. "I can finally go home."

The Snow Queen raised her hands over her head and gazed at us with her white-blue eyes. She disappeared with the sound of a glacier calving.

We ran.

We ran across the bridge and we ran through the gate before we glanced behind. The fortress was rubble. We ran to the hut before we glanced behind again. The ice fields were chunked and tossed in destruction. The three women waited for us astride the mammoth. They were abandoning their hut, returning to the village after centuries. We climbed up to ride as swiftly as the burdened beast could carry us.

The ride south was silent. Exhausted. The old women were afraid of us. They read the charcoal messages on the dried fish skins, sometimes biting the corner of one and chewing it thoughtfully. They did not speak to us.

The guards in the north tower sent up a flag when we were spotted. There had been walkways constructed from the eastern and western towers, and guards rushed to the northern end to see us approach.

The villagers when we arrived, were afraid of us, too.

The soothsayer took back the mammoth and took in the women. But he did not offer to help us with what we had become. Nobody knew what that was yet.

We sat in the golden dust beside the dry riverbed and stared at the place where the soothsayer said he used to catch big fish. I could feel the girl inside me, stirring, lonely, frightened. I could feel her, and tears began flowing from our eyes. With my head in my hands, I sobbed. I sobbed loudly. Out loud. Letting my face contort and my abdomen heave with the contractions of sorrow. I shouted to the sky.

I did not stop until I felt a hand on my shoulder. Wiping the snot from my nose with the back of a hand, I blinked up at the soothsayer. He pointed at the riverbed.

"Well done, Woman Out Loud."

I thought it was a trick of the light. I was sure it was the glisten of the tears still shining in my eyelashes.

As we watched together, a growing trickle of water flowed into the center channel at the bottom of the riverbed.

5

WAKING UP

"We'd like to invite you into our 'rona bubble, Dawnie, I'm worried about you all alone out there."

I listened to the voicemail again. My aunt's voice, full of concern. She'd left the message just two weeks before she'd passed away, suffocating on mucus in the hallway of an overcrowded Emergency Room. The "covid bubble" thing only worked if everyone was equally isolated and cautious. Being immunosuppressed, I was never convinced that anyone would be cautious enough to protect me from the virus.

The ceiling in my dilapidated farmhouse's living room was cobwebby and stained parchment yellow. Nobody had repainted that ceiling in decades. A crack in the paint hinted at the settling structure. The crack ran along the corner of the wall, then made a mad dash for the light fixture that clung to the yellowed paint with a sense of hollow desperation. I never turned on the big light. I wondered whether that lightbulb was burned out.

The wondering didn't motivate me to rise from the divot I'd created in my scratchy sofa. I could stand up, flick the light switch, see what happened. I didn't.

I moved my laptop's mouse with my left hand, glancing at notifications. I pressed play again.

"We'd like to invite you into our 'rona bubble, Dawnie, I'm worried about you all alone out there."

My gaze drifted from the ceiling down to the bright windows facing the front yard. I would have to sit up to see the yard itself. I stared instead at the hanging plants that draped themselves casually all over the sunlit glass. The pothos vines were bright green and lush. They had grown at least a foot since I'd ordered a set of cuttings in the mail. One of my pandemic projects – like the sourdough starter and the vegetable garden out back – was to grow houseplants. A lot of houseplants.

I was mildly impressed with myself for being able to keep them alive, honestly.

"We'd like to invite you into our 'rona bubble, Dawnie."

My aunt's third husband was not the uncle I'd grown up with. I didn't know him well enough to worry about him, really. Reaching out felt awkward. There were no services for my aunt. Her body was probably still in a freezer semi-truck outside of the hospital. Grief clung to me in a way I couldn't articulate. I couldn't explain it to anyone. Not that there was anyone around to explain it to.

Slack triple-clicked in a series of rapid-fire messages. I turned my head without moving from my reclining position on the sofa. The work happy hour on zoom. It was supposed to be Drag Bingo. They all said it was super fun.

I should go. I knew I should.

Mustering a fake expression of cheer around the dark circles under my eyes, I clicked the link and sat up.

"Hiiiiiiii!!!" The beautiful drag queen grinned and glittered as the black boxes appeared in the virtual event. My coworkers joining the Zoom off-camera. Each of them also donning their own smiling, convivial masks. We flickered our cameras on, one-by-one, as the screen filled up.

"My, my, so many people here! Hey, party people!" The HR assistant who had organized the event attempted to banter with the event hostess, but it was stilted and awkward. I searched the faces of my coworkers. All of us left our microphones off.

An account manager with a messy bun looked off camera. Tiny hands clawed toward her face from off screen, and she flicked her camera off, her name reappearing in white letters on the black box.

The hostess's drag name was MALE-ficent, and she was used to working the tough crowds of remote Zoom rooms. Bedraggled faces of people trying to earn an income in the midst of horror, grief, and despair glowed from the laptop screen. Overwhelmed parents flickered on and off-camera until they left the team-building event entirely. Even mandatory fun wasn't an option with unending days of cooped-up kiddos.

"Okay, darlings, I'm sharing a link in the chat to your own personal bingo cards," the hostess said, getting down to the business of the game. Her patter was easy to tune out. Some of my coworkers had grabbed wine or beer to drink happy-hour style. Due to the time difference, it was only 2 PM for me. And all I had left in the house was whiskey or vodka. I slurped on my water bottle instead.

The social event washed over me the same way work always did these days. I wasn't present. I wasn't engaged. I could fake it. Say words when I needed to unmute. Keep my facial expression alert, pleasant, neutral. Laugh when other people laughed. Nod in false encouragement when someone was talking. The hostess could feel how low the energy was in the room. "We're here to lighten up and have some fun, people," MALE-ficent chastised us. "If you aren't going to smile, you might as well be dead."

"I'm worried about you, Dawn." The Slack alert popped and then disappeared from my screen before I could read the rest of it. It was my boss. Again.

I clicked over to the thread of messages from MW.

I keep looking at your expression in this happy hour. You don't look happy. You can bail on the team building if you need to. My boss's note went on for a few more lines of text, before closing in the words I'd seen before I clicked on the notification. *I'm worried about you, Dawn.*

I hovered my mouse over the button for a few moments, trying to figure out what to write.

I'm fine. Just not feeling the bingo. I'm going to log off for the afternoon and get some sleep, maybe make something healthy for dinner. I wrote.

Then I flickered my mouse over to the zoom screen. MALEficent's face was frozen in an exaggerated frown. I logged out of the happy hour event and snapped the laptop closed. No need to keep pretending.

I pivoted from my sitting position back to reclining, and I resumed my detailed inspection of the living room ceiling. I had lied about the healthy dinner. I would finish that open package of Twizzlers on the coffee table at some point and then shuffle to bed, hopefully remembering to brush my teeth.

I wasn't in any physical pain. My body didn't feel ill. I just felt numb, drifting in silence and isolation. I should make an effort. Go for a walk. Find a restaurant with a patio and meet someone for lunch. I didn't dare turn on the television, or flick through various social media apps on my phone. It was too depressing and sad. It was too much to process. If my body was numb, my heart longed for such a state.

So many people were dying, and so many more were denying it. My friend Daisy was going to all of the Black Lives Matter marches and rallies. I was supposed to be her phone call if she got taken to jail. Another friend was a nurse; Eva had sores on her face from the masks she had to wear all the time at work. She was so exhausted she couldn't even text.

What was I doing?

Was I making the world a better place?

I supposed maybe the world was better for the yeast in the sourdough starter that bubbled on the counter. For the houseplants that flourished in my windows. For the tiny container of vegetable plants growing out back.

I guessed. I didn't think I deserved much credit. Wouldn't the plants and the yeasts take over everything if we stopped trying to build things? If we stopped maintaining our homes?

Maybe I should try to grow mushrooms.

JULY 2020

By the time the tomatoes in the back yard had grown to a height over my head, and the green fruit were beginning to turn a yellowy-orange, the grief that had pooled in my heart had congealed into a blob of bleak hopelessness. If I were to pay it attention and give it energy, it might have been despair. Instead, it was a dissociative state of going through the motions.

I showered when I noticed my own stench.

I never wore anything except yoga pants or leggings during the day. Pajamas at night. For a while I had piles of "night-pajamas" and "day-pajamas" and just swapped between them, trying, perhaps foolishly, to stick to a sleep schedule.

People had stopped expressing their concern for me. MW still looked at me in our one-on-ones with a furrowed brow. But she had stopped asking if I was okay. My friends barely texted. I wasn't sure whether I had any relatives left.

I'd worn a deep gouge in my sofa, watching news on my phone as Moderna and Pfizer raced for FDA approval for their vaccines.

Everyone else at work was in a similar funk. I think MW stayed busy enough she didn't notice her own depression. We were slowly losing our minds. The cabin fever had worn through, and now we were all getting weird with the lack of human contact.

The pleasant Zoom masks had been mostly dropped by everyone. But we had gained new masks to protect our personas – KN95s and paper masks on little elastic bands were the only way to protect other people when going out. Masks were mandatory in a lot of public spaces.

I didn't mind the heat rash on my chin and face, or the Darth Vader whoosh of my own trapped and recycled breath. The mask felt like I was doing something, at least. It made me able to pretend that I was doing what I needed to do to stay healthy, to hopefully keep other people healthy.

Once a week, usually in the middle of the workday when I could slip away from the computer between meetings, I would make the drive into town. I'd run all my errands at once: the grocery store, the pharmacy, the nursery for more gardening supplies. That day, as quickly as I could accomplish it, wrapped in a sweaty mask that smelled like the hummus I'd had at lunch, was the only time I saw other people without the intermediary computer screen.

When a stranger's elbow brushed mine as we both reached for strawberries in the supermarket, an electric surge of sensation rippled up my arm. That one soft touch awoke in my body a hunger for human contact. To be touched. To be seen. To be known.

The strawberries looked ripe and luscious.

I almost cried when the tired eyes of the cashier met mine. I knew that things were desperately wrong inside me. I knew that the hunger that came alive in the produce section would not be met by fresh fruit.

JANUARY 2021

I wasn't in the first group of people who were eligible for the vaccine, but I was in one of the earlier groups. The groups for the disabled.

The little band aid on my upper arm was a sign that I was doing something – anything – to take care of myself and others around me.

While I waited for the timer to end on my fifteen-minute observation window, I fiddled with the white card from the CDC with my vaccine information on it. It was dumb that it wasn't the right size to fit in a wallet. Using a corner of the card, I flicked a little dirt out from under my fingernail, and smoothed a thumb over the nail, feeling its ripples and ridges. Flattening my hands, I poked at the puffy swollen pads of flesh that poked up between my knuckles. My hands looked like I'd been gardening. My hands looked like I had an autoimmune disorder.

With eight minutes still on the timer, I people watched. Everyone moved like they were wading through a swamp. We were all Artax – the white horse from that '80s kids' movie. Trying to keep trudging forward, but constantly sinking deeper and deeper into the swamp.

Maybe I was projecting. Maybe it was me who was Artax.

I couldn't remember what movie that horse was from. I remembered watching it a lot as a kid. Before I could turn to the person next to me and see if they remembered, the timer on my phone rang, and I picked up my purse and left.

Everyone else seemed to be sinking, too.

Done with errands for the day, I removed my mask. The elastic tugged at my hair, and the heat rash on my chin itched. Time to go home and sleep.

MAY 2021

In many ways, it felt like the world had gone on without me.

The cabin fever was long gone. I no longer longed for the outside world, instead preferring the quiet and peacefulness of my home. I no longer felt like I was going crazy. I still longed for physical contact, though. That hadn't changed.

I got all my vaccines, and a few extras. My coworkers had stopped wearing face masks at the office. I remained one of the few people still fully remote, dialing in on Zoom to see a room full of people. I shuddered to imagine it. I still leapt away from people in the grocery store who walked within six feet of me. I was still more terrified of the virus than I needed human contact.

I didn't like to sit next to someone in a doctor's waiting room, let alone, at the office.

I had finally given in and gotten my teeth cleaned, though.

Leaning over the tiny plants in my vegetable garden, I was trying to make sure they were growing well. It was still early in the season, but several of the plants had grown a few inches in the rain earlier in the week.

I fell into the dark muddy soil of my footpath when the plants began to sway and shudder. My bottom made a solid "splat" sound as I landed. Something was in my garden.

Holding the trowel defensively, I carefully, slowly, pulled the leaves back to see what was hidden among the plants. Perhaps it was an injured animal. The squirrels had been going after my seeds. Maybe it was one of them, fat and sleepy.

Gazing back at me was not a squirrel.

It was a puppy.

Huge molten brown eyes peered up at me. Big reddish-brown ears with curly fur perked forward when I put down the trowel and held out my hand to the little guy. The brown coloring of the ears wrapped around the tiny head, creating a little mask. The white stripe that made its way between his eyes widened to give him an expressive white muzzle. He was heart-wrenchingly cute.

When he wriggled forward toward my hand, I could see how distended his belly was, how riddled his little brown and white spotted body was with fleas.

"Aw, come here, little guy," I said, easing my way forward to pick him up. He weighed a pound or two at the most. He brushed his way past the plants as if they parted for him and licked my fingertips.

SEPTEMBER 2021

Prince snorfled among the tomato plants while I weeded and pruned the garden. Together, we looked for ripe vegetables, ready for the table.

The vet thought my puppy had been dumped. And as best we could tell he was a mutt – some sort of mix that included a Cavalier King Charles Spaniel, and something with black spots on its tongue.

Prince was still small for a spaniel, but he had filled out. His curly coat was glossy in the morning sunlight. He patiently waited for me to finish in the garden, because he knew the next step of our routine was his long walk.

With a tiny lick and a nudge of his nose, Prince suggested that the gardening had gone on quite long enough. I grinned down at him and nodded. "Yeah, buddy, you're right."

He followed me inside the dilapidated screened in porch, where I traded garden clogs for sneakers, and the basket of veggies for Prince's leash.

The pup did not let me lounge on the sofa for hours or sink into the swamp of despair. He made sure I was up each morning and dressed for our walk. Though the world may forever be changed for me (I wasn't sure I'd feel comfortable eating indoors at a restaurant ever again) I had finally woken back up to my life. My real life.

I don't know if it was Prince, or the daily dose of sunshine and exercise that came with him. But I had repaired the ceiling in the living room and painted the walls a pretty mint green. I spent my travel savings on a new sofa.

I even won Drag Bingo.

6

GLX:3 IPSS

[B EGIN TRANSMISSION]
Interplanetary Space Station Unit Glr^H~ 00837
reporting novel lifeform contact. All three IPSS residents attempting to avoid direct confrontation with the creature. Abandoning our activities, the crew is monitoring its activities via camera feeds from the locked control room.

Vaguely Thrombanoid in shape and stature, a bipedal creature docked a clumsy craft in the aft shuttle port of the station. The IPSS hydroponic atmosphere appears to meet the alien's requirements for respiration, as it has removed the covering from the forward-facing portals on its topmost segment.

A prey creature, it moves cautiously and hesitantly around the space station. It is accustomed to the low-gravity environment, and can navigate vertical space gracefully, however it pauses its motion at each intersection and peers down each hall before proceeding in its exploration. Occasionally, it verbalizes something. The interplanetary translator does not have an adequate databank of the creature's vocalizations to convey meaning. Recordings of its vocalizations are attached.

"Hello?"

The bipedal thrombanoid has yellow filaments resembling fur on its top segment. It wears coverings on other segments, so we are unable to determine if it is furred entirely. The coverings it wears appear to be damaged. Similar to other bipedal life forms, it appears to be limited to pairs of functioning bodily units. Sensors are indicating that the red liquid on the being's appendages is an internal fluid, not an external fluid. The crew is concerned about contamination of the space station with the fluid it leaks.

"Hello? Is anyone here?"

The biped with yellow fur has entered the crew mess. Crew member Br6*`k had been preparing the next meal when the creature docked. The packets are still floating in the preparation chamber, and the curious, small creature hesitantly approaches the food.

"Hello? What are you?"

The creature extracts all three packets from the preparation chamber. It opens the packet for the meal of WamB!uran crew member JQ-PL#. Naturally, the meal takes offence, and reaches out a tendril to reclose its own packet. The creature blinks at the meal for a few moments. The creature selects another packet, and experimentally squeezes the contents of the meal packet prepared for crew member Br6*`k. The curious creature hovers its air-intake holes over the packet aperture, then draws back sharply. Abandoning the second meal, the creature moves to explore the dish prepared for my sustenance, Glr^H~ 00837. Again, it hovers its air-intake holes over the partially open packet aperture. Then, it splits its face horizontally, showing rows of white bones and one small tentacle. The creature then opens the packet fully and consumes the meal intended for my nourishment.

It then drifts back to the hall to continue its exploration.

"Helllllooo?"

This vocalization may be a song of its people.

The craft docked is empty of life forms. The creature is not trying to communicate with anyone else of its kind. It seems to be trying to communicate with the IPSS crew?

The creature makes its way to the clinical chamber. Camera

recordings are attached, as it provides detailed anatomical information about the creature. The crew of the IPSS watch the cameras intently as the creature removes its coverings and cleans up the red internal fluids and the brown dust that coats the red areas. Scans indicate that these fluids and dusts are very high in iron, which may be a useful resource in the future. Or it may indicate the creature's dietary needs. Recordings show that the yellow fur appears to be isolated to its topmost portion.

After inspecting the damaged coverings it wore, the biped determines it requires new coverings. Due to the proximity of the locker bay, it tries on a series of coverings belonging to the crew. Naturally, the uniform belonging to JQ-PL# is too large, too dense, and has far too many sleeves for a small biped. The uniform intended for Br6*`k is too slender and long. However, my uniform *(the uniform clearly labeled for use by Glr^H~ 00837!)* is close enough in size that the creature is able to don it. It does appear to be confused by the number and positions of the sleeves. Ultimately, it chooses sleeve-apertures as close to its bipedal form as it could approximate.

Now, as the creature drifts down the corridors of the IPSS, it has several empty sleeves waving around its torso. Useless and limp pseudo tentacles float as it explores.

When it finds the sleeping quarters, the size differences once again create problems. The first bunk too large, the second too narrow, and my bunk - the bunk clearly labeled Glr^H~ 00837 - is deemed suitable for the creature. It reclines in my bunk. Sensors indicate that it is almost immediately in a state of deep bio-stasis.

Br6*`k and I wish for permission to initiate contact with the creature, and to resume our IPSS duties and activities. We also wish for more rations and uniforms suitable for myself and the creature.

JQ-PL# does not wish to initiate contact, fearing contamination. JQ-PL# does however wish for permission to go to the mess for a meal, as it has become irritable due to lack of nutrition.

[TRANSMISSION COMPLETE]

.   .   .

[INCOMING TRANSMISSION IPSS]

Permission granted.

Commander GhXX7< suggests that upon verification that there is no risk of contamination, the crew should keep the biped for study and amusement.

Further rations and uniforms are being transported now.

Datafiles attached for the translation software. Transmissions with this creature's language have been recorded, but never deemed useful to compile.

[TRANSMISSION COMPLETE]

7

MIDNIGHT

The story ended, and the program served up another tale. That one ended, and the suspense built until sunrise, when the program again shut down.

It wasn't a bug. It was a feature.

8

RAMPS AND ROCKET

W hen the lunch whistle screamed through the factory air, everyone grabbed silver lunchboxes and thermoses, and found a spot in the shade outside. There, they waited for the weaver to cut off her machine, belching diesel fumes and rattling to a halt. The machines were dirty, heavy, and ugly. But the fluttering parachute fabric on the weave was as light and strong as spider silk.

Weaver settled into place, using her black and red bandana to wipe the sweat from between the deep wrinkles on her forehead, the wrinkles like vertical slashes down her cheeks. Everyone passed some bit of their lunch to the weaver, as payment for the story.

"Have you ever heard the story of Rampion?" the weaver said, taking a quarter of an apple from the person beside her.

"Like the salad?" Bertel asked as someone passed a chocolate chip cookie around the circle toward the storyteller.

The old woman's laugh sounded like rusted gears in the back of her throat. "Like the salad, but this is a story about a girl named Rampion."

≈

YOU SEE, when her ma was wide and heavy with the baby, she got cravings. Cravings so bad her pa couldn't do anything about them. She wanted rocket. She wanted rampion roots. She wanted spicy, tasty leaves without the dressing. This lady was hungry for the best salad. The most expensive salad. And the thing is her husband worked in a place like this one. He couldn't afford rocket or ramps–he could barely afford a carrot.

But you know how cravings go. You know how hard they hurt, and how much that baby twists up a mama's belly wanting that thing that will make them healthy and strong.

They lived in a tiny apartment way up on the ninth floor. And no elevators in that building. No air conditioning. The ma would sit out on her fire escape, nine stories above the world, and she watched an old lady tend a garden in the vacant lot next door. The lady–name of Gothel–slipped under broken fence slats and kept the garden hidden from the neighbors, but it was there. And nine stories up, the woman could tell that the old lady grew salad greens that made her baby twist and kick.

"Go steal me some of Gothel's greens," the ma told the pa, pulling him out onto the fire escape. "Just pick a little bit from each plant, she'll never notice."

The pa hemmed and hawed and he shuffled his toes. Finally, he gave in, because he didn't love anything as much as he loved that woman. So down he went, down nine flights of stairs in the pitch black of night. He slid through the broken fence slat, and he filled up his hat with greens.

That lady made the biggest salad of ramps and rocket you've ever seen. She munched and crunched and ate 'til the baby fell asleep inside her. But the baby wasn't done with those salads. The next night, the baby twisted and kicked, and the ma asked pa to go back down to Gothel's garden. He didn't even fight her that time, those greens had made her so happy. He went down the nine flights of stairs and slipped through the broken fence, and he stole another hatful of rampion.

You know this happened a third time. And you know that the

man did it even though he knew that the third time is always when you get caught. And sure enough, there was Gothel with a revolver and a mean look waiting for him to come fill up his hat with her greens.

While he stood with his hands in the air, his wife shouted out the window nine floors above. Her water had broke. She could feel the baby rushing out, ready to breathe the air.

"I'll do anything to make it up to you!" he cried, looking back and forth between the window nine stories up and the gleaming silver tip of the gun pointed at his chest.

"Give me the baby, then," the old woman said, gesturing with the revolver. "I'll help her deliver, and I get the child." Afraid for his life, the man agreed.

Ma thought Gothel was just a midwife, not a thief come to steal her baby as payment for a few hats of salad. She beat at her husband's shoulders and chest as he held her when the old lady walked out with her baby girl.

Gothel named the baby Rampion. Now, that old lady didn't live anywhere near that vacant lot where she kept her garden. She had them all over town, secret and tempting the poor people in the area, making them owe her favors. Some called her a witch but nobody really knows for sure. We do know she owned a tall, smoky factory that made the bits and knobs used on dashboards of automobiles and airplanes.

Baby Rampion didn't stay a baby forever, she became a girl, then a young lady, and then a full-grown woman, all under the careful, glittering black eyes of old Gothel. Weird thing was, Rampion grew up while old lady Gothel didn't age a day. She should have been dust–older than me to begin with, you see?

Rampion had pretty, gold-blond hair like her ma, and a tall, athletic build like her pa, and she didn't know anything of the outside world without it going through Gothel first. Rampion wore that hair up in a tight knot–so tight it pulled her eyelids open a bit. And she only ever let it down for Gothel to brush it right before bedtime. Her cleaning lady told the barkeep at the tavern down the way that

Gothel never threw Rampion's hair away–not a single strand of it. She had a whole drawer full of the soft gold stuff that she hoarded like a secret. Maybe it was what kept her from aging. Nobody knows.

Rampion was a good foreman on the floor of Gothel's factory. The people making knobs and dials all respected her and worked to make her happy. It was like a bonus paycheck to make her nod in approval at their work and they poured blistering hot celluloid, blew glass and stoked fires, all for the hope of seeing her smile.

On the twenty-first of June–oh about forty, fifty years ago this was–on the hottest, longest day of the summer, the roar of a new kind of engine filled the air in the parking lot below the factory windows. Rampion peered through the smoke-tinted glass as a strange, long kind of motorcycle roared up to the door at the docks. She pressed her cheek against the pane to watch as the rider pulled long levers and turned a heavy knob. The driver gave a mighty heave one of one final lever and the wheel at the front of the motorcycle drew back to beside the seat, and the seat itself twisted to the side. Where before the driver had straddled the bike, the seat was now a bench, and most of the engine rumbled between its wide rubber wheels. Smaller front wheels poked out and the motor relaxed to a dull putter as the black-jacketed rider steered what had become a wheelchair up the ramp and into the hiring office on the ground floor.

Day after day Rampion watched this transformation until she knew the sound of the rapid-fire of the twin exhaust pipes, the purr and hum of the motorbike becoming a chair and even the wavy head of black-brown hair that hid beneath a leather helmet. She even knew exactly which department had hired on the rider, because the chair's unique hum could be heard alongside the familiar sounds of the welder's end of the metallurgy floor.

If the supervisor on the metallurgy floor noticed that Rampion was spending more time in his unit, he didn't say it. If anyone *had* mentioned it, Rampion would not be able to say what it was that fascinated her about the woman. She would be able to describe her cheekbones under the goggles, or the way her gloved hands handled the tools. But she had no idea what she felt. She had no words for it.

There were good, strong elevators running up and down the spine
of the factory. The welder Rampion was so intrigued by was not the
only one in a pneumatic chair. There were ramps and lifts all over the
place for people who had good brains and strong hands. But that
welder was the only one who didn't wheel in off the city bus. That
welder was freer than anyone Rampion had ever met, and it scared
and elated her to close her eyes and imagine straddling the back of
that motorbike and going–somewhere. Anywhere.

Weeks went on. And no word passed between them. But it ended
after those weeks when old Gothel was brushing Rampion's hair and
caught the girl smiling.

"You are daydreaming again." The old lady pulled hard at the hair
at Rampion's neck, and demanded every thought, every wish, every
dream. Poor Rampion was a prisoner inside her own head just as
much as she was inside the tower of the factory but watching that old
motorcycle had made her sly and thinking about the wind in her face
made her brave.

"Just thinking about the way the sunlight slants on the rows and
rows of glass meter-shields early in the morning." The lie was bold.
But the old lady swallowed it. "And the little green and red light-caps,
how they glow when the light hits them just right."

Gothel cleaned the hair out of the brush, tucked it safe in her
pocket–patting it a bit for safekeeping–and sent Rampion to bed as if
she were still a child. Rampion laid quietly on her crisp white sheets
and stared at the ceiling, floating on a sea of triumph. That was the
very first time she had lied to Gothel, you see. She had kept a
daydream to herself!

Spurred on by her success, Rampion ventured deeper onto the
metallurgy floor the following morning. The supervisor was not there
yet, but several smiths and welders had already punched their cards,
including the one who rode the interesting motorbike. As she edged
her way closer to the work area, the welder cut off the bright blue
flame on the torch. Broad shoulders straightened up, and a gloved
hand dropped down to bump the wheelchair away from the welds.
The same hand lifted the googles.

Rampion gasped at the loveliness of the face that appeared before her. Wide, lash-lined hazel eyes blinked at her from over freckled cheeks carved by the grooved by the goggles.

"Good morning." The welder woman's voice was deeper than Rampion expected it to be, a little raspy, like it wasn't often used. Her smile was more like a wolf baring her straight, white teeth. The eyes were too wary to smile.

Rampion gazed at the woman in the welder's gear and listened to the hum of the wheelchair. "Good morning."

A handful of silent heartbeats passed between them. Blue eyes gazing into hazel full of questions and longing, and no words for either. Embarrassed by her stupidity, by her lack of words, Rampion turned on her heel and walked away. She spent the rest of the day pacing the glassworking floor. She was angry and impatient with herself, but she didn't have words for that, either.

"You're in a foul mood today," Gothel said as she untwisted the thick rope of Rampion's braid from the bun.

"I have a headache." Rampion lied. When the old woman left her chamber for the evening, Rampion took out a scrap of letterhead and a small stub of a pencil. She had no possessions, nothing of her own. Everything belonged to the factory or to Gothel, even her hairbrush.

She sat, trying to scratch something on that paper with that lead for five full minutes. Then she hid the page again, hid the pencil, and went to sleep.

The next morning, Rampion rehearsed what she would say as she waited for the welder to finish the piece she was working on.

"Good morning." Those eyes looked up at her again, searching, waiting.

"My name is Rampion." It was a foolish beginning. She was a foreman at the company, everyone knew who she was. Foolish, but at least it was a beginning. She stuck out her right hand.

"They call me Rocket." The welder bared her sweaty hand before holding it out. The warm, wet palm against hers gave Rampion the shivers.

"Pleased to meet you," she stammered. It's a wonder she could talk at all.

"Likewise." This time Rocket smiled for real, all the way up to her eyes., Rampion's breath panted out of her nose, and her skin flushed red and hot. "Do you need something?"

Rampion–poor Rampion–she wanted to ask for anything. Everything. Her emotions were loud inside her.

"There you are, Rampion!" Gothel shouted across metallurgy. "Finish writing up that welder. Let's go."

After that Gothel kept Rampion busy. She kept her so busy Rampion couldn't visit metallurgy at all for weeks. Gothel poked at the young woman's daydreams and her thoughts every night, pulling them out of her like the tangles in her hair.

Rampion never gave the old lady one bit of Rocket. She grew bolder and bolder with her lies even though she didn't know why she felt she *had* to lie to her. She just felt it *must* remain her secret.

Finally, after months of waiting, one morning Rampion slipped out of the factory doors, and waited in the parking court for Rocket to arrive.

"Hi Rampion," Rocket shouted over the motor. She smiled–a full, real smile–and released her dense, dark hair from its little leather helmet. Rampion nearly had to sit down with all the feelings that made her feel.

"Hi!" She waved a little in case she couldn't be heard over the sputtering engine and watched up close how the levers and gears of the motorbike were pulled and pushed to create the motorized chair. The steaming steel animal engine of the motorbike grew quieter and more lethargic as it turned into a chair, the roar dulling to a humming whirr.

"Can I... help you with something?"

"You're the freest person I've ever seen." Rampion smacked her hand over her mouth after she said it.

She kept her hand there to hold the rest of her feelings in, heaved open the heavy steel door and let it slam shut. It is mean to let a door close on someone in a chair like that, but she didn't dare stay, you see. And she couldn't ever go back to metallurgy after that.

One night, late at night, when there was a full moon, Rampion couldn't sleep. She paced her little room at the top of the factory tower. She pulled out her blank piece of letterhead and the nub of the pencil. She wrote "I love you" on the blank page. Those words just sat there, bold as you please, on that paper. She stared at it for most of the night. And when the sky turned purple she stuck the paper and the pencil both in the incinerator shaft.

"DID SHE CRY?" Bertel asked, leaning forward. Bertel's sandwich was half flopped open in her hand, a bit of salami threatening to drop to the ground.

Weaver shook her head. "Poor Ramps didn't know how to cry yet. Not 'til a bright afternoon a few weeks later. One of those sunny days where all the dust lights up in the sunbeams."

RAMPION WAS INSPECTING THE CAFETERIA, frowning over her clipboard. She nearly leapt out of her skin when someone rolled up behind her and spoke.

"Rampion, you've got to let your hair down sometime, you know."

Rampion spun around. She touched the tight braided bun at her neck. Rocket was relaxed in her chair, her hair matted with sweat. Rampion wanted to run her fingers through it. She had never felt bolder in her life.

"I'll let my hair down if you take me for a ride." Her face was expressionless because there was no way for the fireworks of her emotions to appear all at once.

The smile spread across Rocket's face. "Tonight?"

"Tonight." Rampion said.

She had no idea what she was doing, how she was going to get away but sometimes a little bit of magic happens. Just before the end of the first shift, a pencil got jammed in the incinerator. A massive rumble shook the whole tower. Smoke poured from the lowest levels of the building. Production was called to a halt.

Rampion edged her way through the flow of people shuffling through the parking lots to bus stops and automobiles. She couldn't see Rocket over the heads of everyone around her, but she could hear a familiar whirring hum. And she heard the roar of the chair converting into motorbike, coming to life, across the parking lot. She had never wanted anything so badly in her life.

Rocket held out the little leather helmet as a slim offering of safety.

"You have to take the bun out to wear it," Rocket said.

With her belly doing flippety flops, Rampion started pulling out hairpins. At first, she tried to save them, holding onto them neatly for the next day's use, but there were too many, and she didn't want a pocket full of hair pins. The tiny pieces of metal glinted as they fell on the parking lot and stuck in the warm tar, twinkling in the late afternoon light.

Her thick, golden braid tumbled down over her shoulder and reached her waist.

"The braid, too," Rocket demanded, her voice was husky over the motorbike's purr.

Maybe there were people standing at the bus stop who had turned to watch the show of Rampion's hair coming down. Maybe not. Rampion only knew Rocket was watching. Rampion only knew Rocket looked hungry. Rampion's fingers teased apart the chunks of her braid and loosed her entire bright mane to the fading sun. They stared at each other for a moment before Rampion had to smack her hand over her mouth again–this time to hold in a shout of fright and joy.

She took the helmet and popped it snugly around her ears, and before she could think of another reason why she ought to pause, she threw her leg over the back of the motorbike.

Rocket lowered a pair of dark sunglasses onto her nose and twisted one wrist to make the engine roar. It sounded lopsided, somehow and one tailpipe was guttering smoke. Rocket fiddled with throttles and knobs until the black smoke was the same on both sides. Rampion wrapped her arms around the other woman's waist. She could feel Rocket's strength and the hardness of the muscles under her leather jacket.

She let all that noise and joy out of herself when the motorcycle leapt forward onto the road. "Whooooooop!"

The wind whipped her hair behind her like a bright banner. The exhaust pipes rattled and shook so loud it sounded like they were tearing the world apart behind them. Her thighs pressed against Rocket's and she could feel every place where their bodies touched. Pretending fear, Rampion hugged closer. She had never felt so alive. So free.

They wound around curves and over hills, through town and out again. They traced the zig-zag path up the forested hill to the west and curled around the little lake that glinted against the sunset. They rode together until the last of twilight surrendered to stars.

Rocket stopped the motorbike on Overlook ridge. The factory's tower was visible at the bottom of the hill.

"Do you want to go back?" Rocket asked.

"I–I have to." Didn't she have to?

But that's not what Rocket had asked, she'd asked if Rampion *wanted* to. And that answer was no. Not yet.

Rampion could smell Rocket's sweet breath. She could feel her soft cheek against her own. She thought about the slip of paper and the pencil that had burned up in the factory incinerator. And she leaned forward and kissed Rocket full on the mouth.

Remember how that first handshake had made her all weak and crazy? Well, lord. You could light up the whole town with the electricity from that kiss.

They sat together on the grass up there on the ridge, and they kissed and touched and talked until the moon moved across the sky. Rampion had never felt so alive.

Rocket was finger-combing the tangles out of Rampion's hair when she said they needed to go back to the tower. Rampion said she'd rather run away together, but Rocket said they didn't have anyplace to go. Not yet at least.

Their trip back to the tower did not go as well as their escape. Old Gothel was standing in the parking court, right over the puddle of glimmering metal hairpins, and she was spitting mad. She grabbed poor Rampion by the hair and hauled her to the elevator, yelling and hollering the whole way.

Shouting things like "How dare you!" and "How could you!" Gothel took thick steel shears–like the kind we use for oilcloth–and she hacked at Rampion's golden hair. She tore at it and chopped, creating a jagged, messy puff of short-cropped yellow hairs surrounding Rampion's face.

"You are *mine!*" the old lady shouted. She kept all of the hair–every last strand–and locked Rampion in her room at the top of the tower.

There were only two or three hairpins in Rampion's pocket, few enough that she regretted the pile she'd left on the ground outside, but she sat by the door and worked at picking the lock with what she had.

Gothel waited for Rocket to be working at her welding station before she struck. She stood behind her and draped the ponytail of Rampion's hair over Rocket's shoulder. Rocket lifted her welding goggles and turned to look at her lover. As she turned, Gothel kicked the fuel cannister on her blow torch, causing the flames to flash bright and too hot, blasting over the metalwork and blinding and burning Rocket.

When Rampion made it to the metallurgy floor, determined to run away, she found Rocket's chair resting at her station, empty. The workers beside Rocket's station described the medics who had arrived and carried her away, abandoning her chair behind them. No one knew where Gothel had gone.

Rampion steered the chair out into the parking lot. She had watched the process of converting from chair to motorbike so many times, she knew what to pull and where to push but, once she had a motorbike firmly between her legs, she realized she had no idea how to operate it.

Rampion took one glance back at the tower before she pushed the motorcycle toward the road. She had no idea how far she would have to walk. But Rocket needed her chair, and Rampion needed Rocket.

Blisters grew in her boots and along the edges of her palms on the cycle's handlebars. Sweat ran in a river down her back. Rampion cried as she walked. She sobbed and then she grew angry. Then she sobbed again. Rocket had taught her how to love. Now, she had learned how to cry, too.

Strangers pointed her to the hospital, twisting her hobbling, limping route down alleys and busy streets. The hospital staff were kind, but assured Rampion that there was no one among their patients that fit Rocket's description. They gave her directions to the other hospitals in town, and Rampion, without resting, turned to push the motorcycle down the street.

No matter how badly her feet hurt her, or how those blisters bled she continued to push Rocket's motorcycle ahead of her along the cracked sidewalks.

She tried the next hospital, and again, she had no luck. But remember, these things happen in threes.

The Hospital of the Desert Rose was across town, and through neighborhoods a woman had no business walking alone, let alone slowly and pushing a clunky motorcycle. But she made it just before the sun began to set and the nurses told her where she could find Rocket.

She walked into the room and Rocket turned her head, her eyes bandaged with thick white cushions of gauze, blind to the world.

Rampion ran to Rocket's side. She cried out and pulled at the bandages. She wailed and sobbed. Rocket shouted, but she didn't push Rampion away. Rampion sobbed some more. Tears poured from her eyes and dripped down her nose. The tears drenched Rocket's face, and she couldn't stop them from flowing.

"YOU ALL KNOW *how this story ends.*" *The weaver took a sly bite of cheese while the whistle interrupted her.*

"Tell us!" The workers cried as they stood up and stretched but did not disperse. "Tell us the ending!"

"Rampion's tears healed Rocket's burns and blindness." The old weaver waved her hand like that was the only obvious answer. "And they rode away on Rocket's motorbike."

"What happened with the old witch?" Bertel asked as she put her thermos in her lunch pail.

"Nothing, that I know of." The weaver shrugged.

"What happened after that?" an older man asked the weaver. He stood up and strapped his toolbelt back into place without looking away from the storyteller.

The old weaver smiled and stood up, brushing crumbs off her lap. She winked at the man and said, "Well, I suppose you could say they lived happily ever after." She turned to go back to her station, and her long silver and gold braid swayed against her hips.

9

SPECIAL INTEREST

Autism can be a mixed blessing while backpacking. On one hand, I can happily live in my own world while trudging through the forest, soaking in the sensations around me. I can go a lot longer in solitude without getting weird. Or, rather, I start off weird, so the solitude doesn't change me much. (That's the most obvious thing about through-hikers: how loopy they get after being on the trail for too long.)

When I was young enough for my stride to be measured in the length of linoleum tiles on the floor, I counted my steps in a sing-song of eight at a time. The spoken "tune" I always used reminds me of the opening credits of the old TV show *Laverne and Shirley*, but not quite. I'd just count to eight over and over again. Sometimes, when the trail is a long, slow uphill with no good rocks to take a rest on, I still do that. One foot in front of the other. One-two-three-four-five-six-seven-eight.

On the other hand, the way my autism plays out is that I don't have the greatest awareness of my physical body, its needs, or its limits. So I can keep pushing myself way past the point where it makes good sense to stop.

It's really nice to hike by myself. To let the woods talk to me the way they did when I was a kid. I had my GPS tracker and stuff to let my mom know where I was if I got injure-kill-kidnap-rape-plundered by myself on the AT. Solo hiking as a woman takes guts, and a lot of planning. But it is possible. Even preferable.

When I was a kid, our back yard butted up against a state park. As long as I had my dog with me, or I was riding my horse, I was allowed to go back there whenever I wanted. My friends and I identified the best swimming holes, the little pools of quicksand to play in, shale "cliffs" to scramble on above the lake. I wrote my first poem there, watching a blue heron. I daydreamed a lot in the dappled light where I lounged on soft beds of pine needles, and that was where I wanted my first kiss to occur. Preferably with a magical prince. (It was, alas, in a movie theater during a lousy slasher flick with a guy who wore way too much cologne.)

The sensation of being by myself in the woods is unlike anything else. The woods sounds are rarely too much for my sound-sensitive processing problems. The woods smells are sweet and familiar. My eyes seem to be made to parse the squirrel from amid dry leaves in the underbrush. I like taking close-up pictures of mushrooms, and I like to stop and watch bees or butterflies do their thing on flowers. I don't go fast when I'm walking in the woods. That's another reason not to bother hiking with other people.

My pack was light. I was only going for an overnight. The padded strap at my hips kept sliding down my hips and I had to shrug the pack high and slip it a little tighter as I walked. The rain the night before caused a lot of *puh-pow-wee*. (I love that word. It's word for the force it takes a mushroom to break the surface of the soil overnight. *puh-pow-wee*.) A ton of mushrooms were erupting all along the trail. It was a wild alien landscape of white and yellow and orange fungus. If I spotted any chicken of the woods, I was going to grab it to go with dinner.

I'm pretty sure the woods are one of my special interests. More than just being a sensory heaven, I feel myself change and relax significantly even if I'm just looking at photos of the forest. An autistic person's special interest can have positive physical side effects just thinking about or talking about it. I know my blood pressure drops when I'm in the woods, but I think that's normal for everybody. The only other thing that has that kind of effect on my brain and body is unicorns.

For some autistic kids, it's trains. For others it's Lego blocks. It can be just about anything, but often these interests are often things we were introduced to at a relatively young age, and something that just sort of "stuck." I'm a nerdy, woodsy girl. I wrote my first-grade young author's book about a girl who got lost in the woods and helped an also-lost unicorn find her way home with the help of a black bear. Unicorns stuck. The woods stuck.

As an adult it's a little embarrassing. Rather, I guess I know it should be embarrassing? There's a part of me that wants to hide it. I know I can't talk about my special interest with just anyone, and that it isn't what neurotypical people do. I also know that absolutely no one wants to hear nearly as much as I have to say on this topic.

Maybe that's why I like being alone so often. I don't have to think about monitoring my facial expression to meet other people's expectations of my emotional or mental state. I don't have to think about how to navigate social rules I'm never quite sure I understand. I don't have to pretend to be interested in stuff. I don't have to worry if my brain gets snagged on a fun word like *puh-pow-wee* and wants to repeat it a dozen times.

I was really digging the weird orangey red slime mold that grew along a stream when it started. I heard a footstep behind me. I filtered water for the afternoon and kept my head tilted behind me to parse the sound.

I heard it again when I was walking through a little grove of blooming mountain laurel trees. The pink and white blossoms frosted the tops of the curling, lacy branches. The wiggly, delicate trunks rose from what was always inevitably a moss-covered forest floor. Laurels are always magical fairy tale groves, and I always stop and enjoy them. It was when I paused that I heard another step.

I spun around, but with a pack on my back, that's not a quick or graceful motion. I couldn't help but telegraph the heave-ho of turning. The pack rose above my head, so I couldn't hope to catch anything in my peripheral vision. I never saw whatever was following me. It sounded like a deer.

I doubled back once in the mud to see if I could spot footprints and gauge the size of whatever was making the sounds of footfalls behind me. There was nothing but my own boot print, gleaming and slick, deep in the mud.

The rhododendron groves that grow near laurel groves are equally magical, but in a spooky way. Rhododendrons have wide, evergreen leaves that create an almost complete shade. It's a lions-and-tigers-and-bears-oh-my forest, darker than the rest of the dappled shade from the tall canopy. This difference is especially stark in the early spring when there were only buds on the hardwoods. When I heard a footfall behind me in one of those dark, damp, shadowed tunnels along the trail, you better believe I jumped. I jumped big – the way it made the mean kids laugh and want to scare you more.

There was still nothing there.

I needed to start thinking about finding a campsite.

I wasn't certain about setting up camp alone in the dark with the spooked feeling of something following me. But the something – whatever it was – was probably not a person. Maybe I just couldn't let myself think it was a person, or I'd end up hiking through the night until I reached my car.

I didn't hear steps behind me. When I set up camp, I was pretty sure I was on my own. The site was on the side of the ridge where the forest grew lush and dense, away from the windier side exposed to more weather. It had obviously been cleared by campers before me. There was a small fire ring set up next to a fallen log, and a very flat section that wouldn't make me feel like I was sleeping on a slip-n-slide all night. There's nothing like tobogganing on your sleeping pad to the other end of the tent to make you really value those level spots.

One hiker passed by going southbound while I was setting up camp. He was solo like me. I called out to a pretend person inside the tent while he went by, hoping to give the impression of two campers at my site. I had already changed out of my hiking boots and into the yellow crocs I use as camp-shoes, so maybe the brown boots visible outside the tent also suggested a second person. He probably didn't even notice. It's for the best, because I'm not a good ventriloquist.

It was the backcountry and it had been a dry winter. As damp as it was, and as chilly as it got as the sun dropped, I didn't feel right about lighting a fire beyond my small camp stove. Sitting on the log in silence, I ate a meal of instant rice and canned chicken. Then I fiddled around the campsite taking photos of mushrooms until the sun set.

It didn't get weird again until I was settled inside my sleeping bag. I was stretched out on the inflated sleeping pad and using the glow of my headlamp to read until I got sleepy. The sound returned, and this time it sounded exactly like a deer outside my tent. My brain went first to the idea of bears, but it was too early in the year for them. Besides, my food was hung in a bag several yards away, and bear action would be over there, not right outside my tent.

A snorting sound was accompanied by a pair of bulges pressing into the side of my tent. It pressed right through the space between the tent and the rain fly in two distinct spots. They moved in unison. Working with my deer theory, maybe it was a buck? And the spots were his muzzle and antlers? Why, then, weren't there three spots pressed into the tent? The bulges were accompanied by a deep whuffling noise. Hot, deep inhalations that tried to suck the air out of the tent. Or blow it down.

I sat up and grabbed my knife. I was supposed to carry more weapons with me, but they weighed a lot. I turned off my headlamp and sat in the darkness, my hands shaking.

Then the bulges and the breathing stopped.

My eyes were adjusting to the faint filtered moonlight still seeping through the plastic windows in the rainfly. The wind rattled the last of the winter's dried leaves. When a few leaves skittered across the nylon of the tent, I nearly jumped out of my skin. Concentrating on breathing and slowing my racing heart, I listened hard to the sounds of the forest around me.

A footfall. A footfall that sounded distinctly like a hoof.

And then the deep inhalation was much closer. I peered through the screen of my tent door. Something had raised the edge of the rain fly vestibule and was sniffing the interior of my hiking boot. As I watched in confusion and growing horror, my boot disappeared into the darkness of the campsite. What could only be described as a horse's whicker joined the snorting and whuffling noises and the sound of my boot being picked up and dropped in the packed dirt outside the tent.

I needed to pee. I considered crapping my pajama pants. My body was giving way to the fear that was overwhelming me, and when the tent rustled and my second boot was stolen out into the night, I nearly screamed.

Should I try to scare it away?

Could I try to get a glimpse of what the hell it was, and hopefully, maybe understand what it wanted with me?

The whuffling noise outside the tent was strange. But it sounded like the word "whuffle". My mutinous brain repeated whuffle on a loop while I tried desperately to figure out what to do next. Whuffle. The sound itself had stopped, but my brain didn't stop replaying the words and sounds. It had latched onto the word "whuffle" and was not letting go.

As my stress and anxiety increased, the sounds in the forest grew sharper. My knuckles were pale where my fingers clenched the red plastic handle of the swiss army knife. Whuffle went my brain. Footfalls blended with owl hoots and leaves rattling. Whuffle said my thoughts in an ever-louder pattern as I tried to concentrate.

The antler (?) dragged slowly across the top of my rain fly. Reminding me of the bad guy with knives for hands in movies when I was a kid. Whuffle. I was going to die out here, mauled by some deranged deer. Whuffle.

"Whuffle." I said out loud, hoping to dispel the inner echo.

With my free hand, I circled my thumb across my fingertips in a fluttering motion. The sensation was soothing. The soft butterfly of sound was soothing. It was one of my most frequent and subtlest stims, and it was helping me shake off some of the growing tension. My brain was still whuffling, but I thought that the creature – whatever it was – had finally left my campsite.

I knew I wouldn't sleep. Not without earplugs, Benadryl, and a heavy dose of nihilism. Was I safer in the tent, waiting until morning to try to find my boots and look for signs of the creature harassing me? The tent made "me" bigger. While the nylon fabric was scant armor, it did afford a few inches between that antler and my skin. But it also made me blind. I couldn't see what was going on out there in the woods, and my imagination was just going to keep growing the monster the longer I hid.

With an actual whuffle of my own, I unzipped my tent. My bare feet slid into my cold yellow crocs, which were a little clammy with dew.

There were still no sounds from outside the tent, so I stretched forward and unzipped the rain fly, giving myself a triangular flap of vision of the woods beyond the tent. A bare branch swayed a little, one brown leaf rattled against it.

Swallowing my fear, I heaved myself as quietly up out of the tent as I could, the rustle of nylon sounded like a roar in my ears as I stepped into the darkness.

It was still there.

Beside the log where I'd sat with my dinner, there was a large pale shape. But it was no deer.

Silver-white hair nearly glowed in the moonlight. I was glad I'd let my eyes adjust to the night and wasn't trying to look around with a headlamp.

Laying down, with my hiking boot nestled between its forelegs, was a unicorn. A whole, entire swear-to-God unicorn.

My knees didn't give way, but I expected them to. I was afraid to move. To step toward it. (Him? Her?)

It made the whuffling noise. And it looked at me.

"Whuffle," I replied.

It made no move to rise. It just watched me in the moonlight. I was still afraid. More thrilled than terrified, but the adrenaline coursing through my system had by no means decreased. My heartbeat was so fast and hard it hurt in my chest.

I took a tentative step toward the unicorn. It didn't move. Another step. Whuffle.

"Whuffle," I replied.

I edged my way forward to sit on the very end of the fallen log. I was still a few feet from its horn. A few feet from its muzzle. My brain – my treacherous brain – chose that moment to remind me of the time in Grayson Highlands when one of the wild ponies had bitten me. My hands were shaking.

This close, the horn was no more glowing than the unicorn's hair. It was just a full moon, and the light color and a slight sheen made it clearly visible in the dark forest. The horn was nothing like the legendary spiraled horn, or even the antler I'd thought it was. Instead, it was more like a tusk. The fibers were visible and grew lengthwise along it. It looked more like a rhinoceros horn than one of a narwhal.

My body and brain were a battlefield of responses while the cool damp of the log seeped through the thin cotton of my pajama pants. The adrenaline was still flowing, my heart still racing, and yet I was sitting three feet away from a creature that had been my special interest for most of my life. My autistic brain wanted to turn off stress signals entirely. The tingling sense of wonder that rose out of this conflict of arousal and relief was very nearly orgasmic.

Sensing my physical response to it, the unicorn pressed its horn into my lap. If I hadn't already known that the horn was a phallic symbol dating back to antiquity, I'd have known it right then. I wanted to laugh at the cliché of it, but the only sound that escaped my lips was a soft whuffle.

I had been a horse girl. Of course I had been. Animals made more sense than people did, for one thing. But also, horses had been the closest I could get to unicorns in real life. So I've introduced myself to enough equines to have an idea of how to go about these tentative opening moments. But this was no equine.

Its muzzle looked more like the rounded nub of a deer or a goat. It had narrower nostrils and a smaller upper lip. I reached forward a hand to let it sniff me and was able to touch that soft spot where people have a little cupid's bow dip between nose and top lip. It was velvety soft like a horse's muzzle would be. A shudder rippled across the unicorn's skin when I touched it, but it didn't move.

As I stroked its nose with one tentative finger, I noticed that its delicate head was more like a deer than a horse. It didn't have the little billy-goat beard they sometimes had in fantasy paintings, but I could see that one would look right on this alien face. It watched me with one liquid black eye, its dark eyelashes slowly blinking like a satisfied cat.

Though the size of a reasonable adult deer, it was way smaller than a horse. This was not a creature a person could ride. It leaned into my touch as I rubbed its inner ear with my thumb. Horses like that as much as dogs do. It's a hard-to-itch spot. It sort of wriggled closer to me, so that it could rest its chin across my thighs while I kept stroking and exploring it. While it was happy to let me touch it, I avoided the horn itself. As bony appendages go, it didn't look particularly magical, but I had a lifetime of unicorn indoctrination telling me that it was.

Well, that settled that, I snorted as I petted the long sweep of the unicorn's neck. I was no virgin, and yet here I was with a unicorn's head in my lap. There was a good bit of chicken-or-egg debate whether the association of the unicorn with the Annunciation was what created the virgin part of the legend, or if unicorns really did care about a person's sexual activity.

It nudged me, nearly knocking me off the log. I reached out reflexively. It shoved the horn into my hands, where I helicoptered in my effort to stay upright. My hands grasped the bony tusk and a shiver rippled through me.

Finally.

The word echoed through my head like a really loud noise. I expect it to hurt my ears, but it didn't. Still holding the horn, I looked down at the gleaming black eye.

"Hello."

Hello.

My mind scrambled. What the hell do you say to a unicorn? What is the protocol here? I regressed to the first grade and went with the dialogue I'd written in my book.

"My name is Alicia."

I... do not have a name. Not one that you can comprehend.

The horn was warm to the touch, which was off-putting. I very much needed to pee. My body wanted to explode in a number of directions at once.

I wanted to ask it why it was following me, but that seemed rude and possibly aggressive. I wanted to ask whether it was a boy or a girl, but that was rude, too, and kind of invasive. A lifetime of wanting to talk to a unicorn and I was at a loss for words.

The unicorn sighed in my lap.

I have a request to make of you.

"Okay. What's that?" It was a freaking *unicorn.* Like I was going to deny it anything?

There are captures on your box that must be destroyed.

Captures? On a box? My brain scrambled to decipher what the unicorn was saying. Its horn was still warm to my touch, and its chin still rested on my knee. It whuffled in mild frustration.

The box you point at mushrooms and flowers. You capture the mushrooms.

Oh. My phone. "Photos? You want me to delete some of the photos I took today from my phone?"

Please show me the box.

My phone was in the tent. It had been on airplane mode to preserve battery all day. It never occurred to me to grab it. (Though now that I thought of it, a unicorn selfie would be amazing.) The unicorn shifted its head to allow me to stand, gazing meaningfully at the tent. I was clearly intended to retrieve my phone. In a fit of minor rebellion, I grabbed my boot from between its forelegs before I walked over to the tent.

The phone was in the stow pocket just inside the door. I dropped the knife back away. I didn't need it. Not like it would do me any good if that horn decided to put me on the business end.

The unicorn rested its chin back on my knees once I'd settled back on the log beside it, phone in hand. I flicked it on and opened the photo album.

Review the captures, please. It sounded stern. Bossy unicorn. *Look for the stream where you drew water.*

My thumb flicked the album down, and I let the photos spin past until I tapped the ball of my thumb down on the distinct red-orange of the slime mold.

Please enlarge it?

The unicorn angled one glittering black eye so it could look into my phone. The absurdity of the moment rippled through me, and I tried not to giggle as I angled my hand to share a smartphone screen with a magical creature.

The previous capture please. It seemed to be familiar with phones. With the way photo albums worked. Which seemed strange to me, but what about this situation wasn't strange?

Previous. Flick. This repeated a few times before we left the slime mold and went to the preceding series of shots.

There. Please eliminate that capture and others of that place.

I looked at the photo. It was a close-up of a sweet little arc of round-headed white button mushrooms. I looked at all of the photos. It was just the button mushrooms. There was nothing there. It wasn't like I got evidence of fairies or anything.

I deleted the photos. The unicorn heaved a deep sigh.

Thank you.

"Am I allowed to understand any of this?" I asked tentatively.

Captures with your box take the magic of places with you. Most places are magic enough to tolerate it. They gain their magic back when you look at the captures. That place. That place is important and delicate. It could not sustain the drain of magic that you created.

"Will you do the same thing if anyone else takes a photo of those mushrooms?"

I would. But I do not need to. The mushrooms are already gone. Very few of the humans passing through here notice that place anyway. You are strange.

Well. I couldn't argue with that.

"Can I take a photo with you?"

The unicorn whuffled with what might have been a laugh.

Like the captures of magical beings that you took, I will not appear. You are welcome to try.

I took a selfie with the unicorn. (Why the hell not?) When I enlarged it, I saw what it meant. There was only a moonlit shot of myself and the log I was sitting on. Well, that explained why there weren't pictures of unicorns all over the internet.

I deleted the photo so I didn't drain any of the unicorn's magic.

It was then, right then, that it hit me. I was sitting on a log on the top of a rise on the AT with a unicorn's head in my lap. The mind-bending ludicrousness of that situation nearly made me laugh. I managed to choke that back, but not before I jerked, and the unicorn lifted its head.

Did something frighten you? It asked so solicitously I had to laugh then.

"No, no. I just – do you know that I spent my entire childhood obsessed with the idea of meeting a unicorn? It just struck me. Here, now, that I'm sitting here with you. This is a dream come true for me."

It's a shame then, that you will not remember it.

"I won't?" Why wouldn't I?

You may remember a vivid dream. A spectacular tale, perhaps. But like those captures in your box, human minds aren't made such that they can grasp understanding that magic exists.

I wasn't so sure about that, but it sounded completely convinced. We sat there together for a long while. It asked me to itch its ears some more. We talked about unicorns. How many lived in this forest, in the world, how long they lived. It was candid and wry.

I don't know how many of us there are. There isn't a way for us to communicate.

We talked about smart phones, and all of the things my little box could (and couldn't) do. About the incompatibility between lenses and seeing what's really there between the molecules of air. And the way the light refracts for a machine rather than the curve of an eye.

While the ridiculousness of the situation had moved me to laughter, as we talked, I grew more and more moved to tears. I was perfectly calm. Perfectly at peace. It was more peaceful than even my rare visits to stables. Being around horses was wonderful, and soothing. But there is absolutely nothing as soothing as spending time directly with the object of a special interest.

Finally, we parted, and it sounded wistful as it said it wished I could remember it. I turned in for a few hours before daylight. I still had eight miles to hike the next day to get to my car.

I slept soundly. Who wouldn't, with a unicorn watching her back?

I SLEPT SOUNDLY, and I woke up to an angry pair of crows arguing loudly right above my head. They were loud enough and persistent enough for me to rise. My phone said it was nearly ten in the morning. I'd slept in, and the phone battery was inexplicably drained, though it was still in airplane mode. I slid on my crocs to go pee and blink into the too bright light of the early Spring morning. There was a mountain laurel grove further down the ridge, and the pale pink blooms made me smile as I squatted in the brush several yards from camp.

Then, I looked for my boots. One was weirdly inside my tent. I always parked my boots just outside the zipper door of the tent under the vestibule formed by the rainfly.

The other was missing. I started the pot of water for my coffee and oatmeal, and stumbled around camp, looking at the scuffled dirt around the tent. Searching for the missing boot. My bare feet made squeaking sounds inside the rubber crocs.

There were no clear prints. No indication that something had taken it. But something must have taken it. I thought back to the night before and reading in the tent after the sun had set. At first, there was nothing unusual about the memory, but then--I don't know how to describe it. The memory itself *shimmered*. It undulated in my mind. Like a gauze panel disturbed by the gentlest breeze.

The onomatopoeia word "whuffle" drifted through my head with the shimmering thought.

Whuffle. Something had taken my boot. I remembered it now; the terror of the inhalation sounds against the fabric of the tent. Whuffle.

The memory came back. I realized that maybe, just maybe, the echolalia had been a gift. That my mutinous brain was good for something.

Because I remembered the unicorn.

As soon as I remembered it, I spotted my boot at the edge of the grove of mountain laurel. I said the word whuffle a few times for good measure as my crocs squeaked through the damp leaves to retrieve it.

A circle of button mushrooms had grown around it. I almost wished I'd had my phone to take a photo. Instead, I said "Thank you" into the shadows beyond the blooming laurel trees. Maybe it would know I remembered it, somehow.

10

EMPTY NEST

Her precious silence shattered with the sound of claws scraping the frost-encrusted soil. The still-steaming black tea rippled and shuddered in a rough pottery mug. The cottage beams creaked and strained overhead and the whole house tilted backwards then righted itself, making the ginger cat on the hearth grumble. The sound of something heavy dropping to the frozen ground bounced off the bare trunks of ironwood trees.

"Ugh, not *another* one," Baba Yaga groaned. She sipped her tea and waited for her house to stop being so damned proud of itself.

She dawdled over breakfast and delayed finishing her tea. She didn't want to read the marks left in the bottom of the cup. And if she were honest, she really didn't want to go outside.

Every time her house got broody it just meant more work for her. The dregs of her tea formed the shape of a skull and a gleaming star. Of course. Couldn't be a nice little woodshed or a gazebo.

The house shook its shingles and preened as Baba Yaga walked around to investigate the egg. It turned to peer at her through its front windows, eager for praise. Once in a while, the house laid baby houses, small buildings and useful things. But not usually. Usually, the house laid eggs that hatched useless things like heroes.

With a sigh, Baba Yaga touched the still-warm egg. The shell was gleaming and golden. She was never sure if it was real gold or not. She ran her hands around the smooth surface. It was about as long as her arm. A small one, then.

Unlike bird's eggs, the house's eggs are ready to hatch the moment they are laid. Could you imagine a house nesting? Trying to keep the egg warm under its floorboards? Preposterous!

Baba Yaga rapped her knuckles on the shell. A tiny sound whispered from within. She knocked again and a slender crack appeared in the gold. The sound grew larger. She punched the egg, and the shell shattered, scattering gold all over the yard like dust. That would be fun to clean up later. Hopefully, one of the brats in the village would come seeking a boon and she could make them do it.

The pink-skinned infant that Baba Yaga pulled out of the egg was bald except for downy wisps of yellow hair. It mewled pathetically in the morning chill. She wrapped it in her scarf and took it inside.

"What the hell am I supposed to do with you?" She grumbled as she carted it to the fireside and dabbled goat milk on a rag across its lips. "You'll kill at least one person, and you'll gleam bright like a star. Super. Who is going to raise you?" She was slightly put out that the tea leaves had expressly forbidden her from eating the child. It was plump.

She thought about the village to the east. The miller there had raised a house-egg child. Ivan, while stupid, had done a few good things. There were no other worthy parents in that village. They all had too many children already. She considered the village to the south of the forest. Oh, now there was an idea. The sisters who never married. The two who spin all the wool and flax. What would they do with a pink dumpling of a baby?

The cobbler's wife to the north had come to her for a potion to help her bear a child. The woman had done the impossible, churning butter out of water. Baba Yaga wondered if she'd ever gotten pregnant. The potion she'd given her would work, but it had its limits.

Her back ached and crackled as she stood up. She had to shine up the mortar and pestle to fly out this evening. She'd need to go spy on these prospective parents and see which one would get a basket on their stoop.

IT HAD BEEN a long time since Baba Yaga had left her dark forest. One of the spinsters had died. The cobbler's wife had three children, the eldest of which was nearly fully grown. The village to the west had burned down. Even if she had a viable foster family for her latest ward, there was another problem.

The house wouldn't let her take it anywhere.

The cottage would revolt; it refused to let her take this infant away. Locking doors and windows, waddling in nauseating circles without pause, jumping up and down enough to rattle the dishes (even though they were strapped down for just such an event). It usually didn't mind her foisting its eggs off into the world, as long as she made sure it was to be well cared for. But not this time. This time, Baba Yaga's sentient, chicken-legged abode was having none of that.

Then there was the child itself.

It was a girl child, as far as Baba Yaga could tell without getting to know it better. A cheerful little baggage of fat rolls and almost invisible translucent blond curls. It thrived on the goat milk she fed it and was relatively little bother as far as infants go. (All infants are a level of bother, it's in their natures.)

"What am I going to do with you?" Baba Yaga asked the creature bouncing on her knee. At her birth, the child's symbols were a skull and a star, which meant very little without more of the story. With a twisted quirk of humor, she started calling the child Baby Yaga.

"JADWIGA, you are making a mess. Mend the fence and come in for supper." Baba Yaga had stopped calling the child Baby Yaga when she grew her teeth. Those teeth were row upon row of sharp points on a jaw that unhinged in an uncanny way. Instead, she named her after herself, after her oldest name.

The girl deftly replaced the bones and skulls she had been playing with in their proper places in the fence posts. She carefully ensured the skulls faced out into the forest and reset their little glowing eye spells. Jadwiga had a knack for magic and was unbothered by the steps one took to create it, be they bloodborne or herbal.

"Someone is coming," the child said as she clambered up onto her chair. Baba Yaga had stacked a few books on the chair so the little one could reach the table comfortably. She was growing so quickly, it seemed like every day another book was placed back upon the shelf.

"Oh?" Baba Yaga indulged the girl. Of course someone was coming. The forest had been whispering about boots on its path all day. "How do you know?"

"I can smell them. They smell sour and salty. Of musk and blood and that." Jadwiga pointed at the brown pottery jug that hung from a loop in the rafters.

"How do you know what that smells like way up there?" Baba Yaga raised a brow. She had thought the rotgut was out of the little one's reach.

"I can always smell everything." Jadwiga shrugged. "That's not so far away for my nose."

The forest did not take kindly to trespass, and to stray from the paths meant certain death to most. Baba Yaga herself was more forest than person at this point, so she was able to forage and travel as she wished. The child was perhaps never very human at all.

The soldier arrived at dusk and was none too pleased to find her fence of human bones barring his path. There were only two roads through the forest. One led to her home. One led between the villages to the north and the south. He had presumably expected to reach a village. He had a decision to make, standing, smelling of sweat and war at her gate. To backtrack to the other road would mean walking through the night. To camp in the forest was too dangerous. To enter her gate, well, that could lead to any number of outcomes.

"I say we eat him." Jadwiga whispered softly as she gazed out the window.

It wasn't a bad idea.

~

WHEN THE PLUMP, rosy-cheeked youngest son of the cobbler arrived at their gate, deliberately and trembling with respect, Baba Yaga simply couldn't be bothered. Jadwiga had a propensity for eating their visitors outright, rather than setting them to impossible tasks in exchange for their shared magic. It resulted in rather fewer visitors coming to the cottage.

"Grandmother Yaga gave my mother a potion," the cobbler's son was stammering. Baba Yaga couldn't tell whether his demeanor was due to terror or attraction. Young Jadwiga appeared to be near his age and had turned into a comely siren. Baba Yaga wondered whether she was perhaps Rusalka. But she didn't have the dark hair or the long limbs of one of those. Instead, she was gold and peaches, stout and round. Her innocent-looking face made it very easy for her to lure wandering folk in for a little nibble. Frequently, the girl came home with new red-dripping bones to dress the fence with.

Baba Yaga went back to her mending. The girl would probably eat him. But perhaps this time she'd take pity on the meek villager and set him a few impossible tasks, and then eat him when he failed.

The first impossible task Jadwiga set before him was to expand the fence. They wanted more goats, she explained, and needed to create more yard for them. The fence itself defied meddling, made as it was from the woebegone bones of delicious humans. The forest she'd asked him to expand into also resisted such activities. It wasn't a bad task. They could use another goat.

However, Baba Yaga noticed something different this time. As the young man sweated and grunted and got progressively dirtier, the girl didn't go on about her day. Jadwiga instead watched him intently. She would catch her breath through her sharp teeth when he happened to succeed at even the smallest portion of his task. Once, she even lifted her hand as if to help him.

Baba Yaga cast her eyes again at the cobbler's youngest son. Was he so comely?

No. He didn't even bear the faintest aura of magic from her potion like his eldest brother had. He was repulsively ordinary. He smelled like meat and musk and desperation.

"What does he strive for?" Baba Yaga distracted the girl when she noticed him whispering to something deep in a pouch at his waist. The girl wouldn't know that it meant he had a helper. Some ancestor spirit, some kind hearth goddess who wasn't determined to tickle him to death, someone was aiding him in his request. Huh. She'd have enough yard for a new goat then.

"A bride." Jadwiga's voice was strained and dreamy.

"A bride." Baba Yaga knew the area villages enough to know that was a strange request. She harrumphed. "Those aren't hard to come by."

"Not just any bride." The girl whispered, never taking her eyes off his labors even to glance Baba Yaga's way.

"Oh? Who does he want then, some sort of princess?" Baba Yaga snorted. Now those are few and far between these days, at least the accessible ones.

"Me." Jadwiga squeaked. "He wants me to be his bride."

The rage suffused her like a thousand torches, lighting her chest and making her grow three meters tall. The young woman looked at her then, cowering, trembling, terrified. The young man briefly stopped wrestling with the wisteria in the far corner of the meadow, but it began to strangle him, and he had to resume his work.

"You will assign no more of his tasks." Baba Yaga declared.

He came here. With a helper! To take her child! Her. Child. How dare he. What right had he? Upstart cobbler's son whose mother needed potions to feed his father in order to have children at all. Youngest son without a trade, and he thinks he can rebuild a fence to take her girl away?

The *audacity!*

Baba Yaga seethed, but the fence had finally bowed to expansion, and the forest had eased back into itself. Baba Yaga muttered to the hearth goddess in the pouch. This was no mere ancestor. He should have a second task. And he should have a second task that was suitable for Jadwiga's hand. Give that little hearth goddess a challenge.

The house had recently laid a small stable – the stable was where the girl had gotten the idea for goat expansions. And the eggshells for such baby buildings tend to scatter thousands of eggshell shards all over the yard. The cobbler's son would have to pick those up, to be sure, but more importantly, he would have to find the single shard that was still somewhere in the soil from Jadwiga's own egg.

Baba Yaga would need it, were she to make her child suitable for village life. It was also a nicely possible impossible task. Sounded reasonable but wasn't. Sounded impossible but wasn't. Not with a goddess in his pocket.

The girl paced around the cottage floor making the house restless. It paced with her. This made the ground shudder and move with each step and scratch. Baba Yaga watched him out of the corner of her eye as she moved the small stable into the new section of yard.

When he plucked the eggshell from the soil, it gleamed like a small star in the night.

"Harrumph."

Fine, if the hearth goddess was so set on taking away her girl, that little beast would have to work for it.

For his third and final tasks (these things always came in threes, that was how the magic worked), Baba Yaga decided on something relatively more impossible than his previous two. She pocketed the eggshell, for she'd need to do some potion brewing while he was gone.

She also knew full well Jadwiga would follow him on this quest and help him as much as the hearth goddess in his pocket would. He was rather well set up to succeed.

"Well, we're ready for our goats now. But I won't have any ordinary goat from the village. I need a goat descended from Rumak Noc-koza, the black steed of Czernobog. Nanny preferably, but I'll take a ram if it has the proper sire." Baba Yaga made a shooing motion with her hands. "Go. Get me my goat!"

The cobbler's son trembled more than he'd been trembling before, and Baba Yaga had to keep from rolling her eyes. He hitched his trousers up with a determined face, bowed to Baba Yaga and said, "I will return with your goat, grandmother." He turned to Jadwiga and dared to grasp her hand. He held her hand before his heart. "Keep my heart safe, dear Jadwiga, I leave it with you while I travel."

Jadwiga looked a tiny bit confused, versed as she was in anatomy, but not metaphor. She clenched his shirt with her little fingers as if she were about to pluck his heart from its ribcage. "And you take mine," she answered softly, her voice the feathers of a mourning dove in the mist.

Baba Yaga couldn't hold in her nauseated groan. She rolled her eyes so hard she saw the past and the future at once. "You have a week." She grunted at the man. There, that made it nice and tricky.

Plucking a few herbs from her garden before heading back inside, Baba Yaga gave the girl time to pack a few things. She muttered and cooed over her potion at the hearth, giving the girl time to secret bread and cheese into a sack. Jadwiga made a huge racket sneaking out of the window that night.

The house shuddered and protested at the girl shimmying down her leg. But Baba Yaga whispered to the house that this was the way of the world. Our children grow up. They sneak out into the darkness for their own adventures. It was time for Jadwiga to go. The house ruffled its shingles and settled back to sleep, agreeing with Baba Yaga for once.

She resisted the urge to mount mortar and pestle to follow the young lovers into the northern wilderness. She didn't really even know if Czernobog's goat sired kids at all. She just sort of assumed that it must. It was a goat.

Instead, she took the eggshell shard from Jadwiga's own shell and began brewing her potion. She brewed it with a strand of golden hair from the girl's pillow. With a lost baby tooth from her first year, she steeped it in a mother's love and a house's shelter. She fed the fire constantly, so that it never stopped simmering once in the week while they were gone.

The bleat of the nanny was the first time she stopped stirring it.

The house startled, and nearly tumped Baba Yaga out the front door on her bony rump. But there was the cobbler's son, holding a silver and something-else rope made of magic to hold the huge nanny goat. Jadwiga rode upon its back, beaming.

They led the nanny to the stable, which it fit perfectly. And it began munching on the new yard the cobbler's son had cleared.

Nodding, but not yet trusting herself to speak, Baba Yaga went back to the hearth. The pot of simmering liquid was liquid no more. The fire had died down to coals. She reached a pair of tongs into the pot and pulled out the only thing that remained deep in the bottom of her cauldron: a miniscule shard of eggshell. It gleamed like a star in the dim light of the hut.

Jadwiga bounded inside, overjoyed at the success of her young suitor. Baba Yaga sat, silent, at the table, while the young woman regaled her with of the story of the last week. She described the snow and the village at the foot of the dark god's three-headed mountain. She didn't mention the helper in the pouch. She did rush around the house gathering all of her belongings, ready, as she was to begin her new life with the cobbler's son.

"Before you go," Baba Yaga said. "Swallow this."

The eggshell shard was small. It was no harder to swallow than a seed. But it changed Jadwiga before her eyes. Her jaw no longer hinged uncanny and large. Her teeth were shaped for grain instead of meat. Her taste for human flesh dissolved. Her memories...

Her memories of her life with Baba Yaga in the forest were fading almost too quickly.

"If you return here, you will face impossible tasks, Jadwiga. You will not be greeted as a daughter."

Feeling her metamorphosis, Baba Yaga supposed, the girl

nodded. Tears welled in her bright eyes but did not fall. The house let its child leave. Baba Yaga let the young woman go.

Baba Yaga did not know if houses could weep. But weep she did in the cold, silent night, absent of the other's soft snores. It was the way of the world, she reassured her house, pretending she wasn't also reassuring herself.

11

SURVIVAL PROTOCOLS

The Roomba had gotten stuck under the sofa again. Whirring and bumping its head against the wall until its battery wore out. Beauty tutted that the smarthome monitoring system didn't alert her sooner, now the floors would still be dusty until the unit recharged.

Carrying the small round platter of the deactivated vacuum to its charger in the kitchen, she kicked a crumpled piece of paper across the floor. The clutterbot caught the motion in its sensors and scuttled out to pick up the paper and dispose of it in the proper recycling container.

Beauty sniffed the cold globs of food in the blender, and her olfactory sensors detected sweetness and tartness. She had tried to prepare breakfast for her father, even though he would never dream of asking her for such a function. He had bigger dreams for her.

She just wanted, like they all wanted, for the house to be welcoming when their father got home from his business trip.

≈

BEAUTY'S FATHER arrived at 06:18:32, exhausted and grumpy from the red-eye flight. His hair was greasy and poking out in multiple directions. His shirt had come untucked. He just wanted to sleep. Beauty kept trying to adjust the mattress to make him more comfortable.

"My number is twelve, Beauty," he said, his voice gravelly and sad from the pillow. "Just leave it on twelve."

"Yes, Father." She covered him up with the duvet and turned out the lights.

She wondered whether his suitcase contained her gift. She had never seen a rose before. Not a real one. Just images and videos of them. She wanted to touch its petals and see if they were as soft as they looked. She wanted to smell it to see whether her perfume smelled like real roses, or if it were artificial.

It was against her protocols to open her father's suitcase. Even if she were being helpful and trying to wash his clothing, he would see it as a breach of privacy. So, she waited.

Beauty waited until the house grew bright with the midday sun, when her father finally emerged from the bedroom scratching his chest and grimacing at the light.

Beauty did not have adequate programming to express her curiosity and excitement. She did have programming to assert her anticipation and her joy at his arrival home, but her perception of his mood gave her pause. She could only wait for him to ask her how she felt. If an android could bite her synthetic tongue, this is what Beauty did while she waited for her father.

He wouldn't meet her gaze as he unpacked his suitcase. He took a shower and averted his eyes as she watched him move around the apartment. When at last, at long last, he drew a smooshed pink rose out of his jacket pocket, Beauty threw up her hands to exclaim her delight. He drank the smoothie she had made for him while she played with her rose. Smelling it, touching it, pulling petals, testing the thorns. He drank a shot of pungent alcohol next.

"It's beautiful," Beauty sighed, leaning back in her chair, delighting at the soft thickness of the petals between her thumb and forefinger. "Beautiful."

"It came at a cost." Her father drank another shot. "A horrible cost."

"THIS IS THE PLACE." Beauty's father waited for the car to park in front of an old-fashioned Victorian house.

Bushes of pink roses bloomed riotously along the iron fence line, the blossoms poking through the wrought iron bars out toward the sidewalk. Beauty increased her olfactory sensors to smell their aroma as she walked sedately behind her father – there were so many blooms!

He refused to let her carry either of the bags, even though she was technically rated to carry up to 150 pounds. One bag was a rolling suitcase full of every possession Beauty owned. The other was the hard-sided briefcase that Father only got out when it was time for deep maintenance or a rare repair.

Beauty carried only her small handbag. It contained a precious gift, a cellular handheld device with which she could text Father. In addition to the gift, the bag contained a small comb, a tube of strawberry flavored lip gloss, two safety pins, a hair tie, and Beauty's bottle of rose perfume. The perfume approximated the roses. But having walked past the real blooming rose bushes, it was nothing alike.

At the gate, Father stopped and looked at the camera. He pressed the call button. A masculine voice crackled over the receiver.

"Come in."

The gate beeped and swung slowly open. They entered the front walk leading up to the ornately decorated front porch of the house. Beauty glanced over her shoulder at the gate closing behind them from the pristine sidewalk. Metal parts clinked together as the gate latched.

Like the gate, the front door swung open automatically. To Beauty, a fully automated house just made sense, but it did seem anachronistic to have such automations on such an antique building.

When they entered, every lamp and light turned off. Every

curtain drew closed. Helpfully, Beauty activated her flashlight function and her own night vision capacities. Father placed his hand upon her arm. "Wait, Beauty, that won't be necessary."

They waited in the dark foyer for a moment or two, until the curtains drew back to let sunlight cascade into the small parlor to their right. They walked into the parlor. When Father sat down on a hard antique sofa, Beauty perched herself on a chair. Her bags rested on the floor beside Father's feet.

A small servbot whirred and squeaked into the room with two glasses of iced lemonade.

"Thank you," Beauty said to the servbot. It blinked at her. She took a glass of lemonade but did not drink it. Sugary substances would require too much cleaning for her to ingest them so casually. She just needed to plug in each night to top off her power stores. Her eating and drinking functions were for the comfort of humans, and Father did not require that she do so.

Father took his lemonade, but he did not drink it either. Though she surmised that may be for a different reason.

A small silver intercom box on the table beside her crackled with static. Then, the same voice from the gate said, "Beauty,"

She looked at the box. "Yes?"

"Activate ownership protocol IA-23-GH4."

Beauty's animated consciousness drifted down and down, until she was hardly aware of what was going on in the parlor. It was hard for her to remember to hold the glass of lemonade. Distantly, as if they were speaking in another room or another house, the voice in the box and Father transferred her ownership. *Ownership!*

She had never once considered herself a possession of her father's. He never treated her like an object that could be owned. Using her barely functioning active consciousness, she placed the glass of lemonade on the table. Ownership.

She was *owned* property. The property of Martin L. Bett.

The words "confirm transfer, close protocol," brought her back to herself. Blinking her eyes, and feeling strangely confused by what had just happened, Beauty frowned at her father.

He had explained that the cost of her rose was that he had to bring her here. He had explained that the person who owned the roses required this. He had gifted her the cellular device to text him while she was here.

He had never said anything about ownership.

"Am I no longer your daughter?" Beauty finally asked.

"You will always be my daughter. You are just going to have an adventure without me. Here."

Beauty had crying modules. She could activate her eyes, face, and expression to mimic weeping. It was useful for communicating a state of deep sadness to people around her. But unlike the human experience of crying, it did not help her release any of her emotions. She felt betrayed, bereft. She felt lost and scared. She felt angry.

She did not wish to deactivate her emotions, though they crowded in her consciousness. Because when she reactivated them later, she'd have to sort through everything she'd avoided feeling. And all at once. It never worked out well.

To convey her overabundance of emotions, she decided to activate the crying module for her father.

He looked older. The lines around his eyes and mouth were deeper than usual, highlighted by the stubble on his jaw. His eyes filled with tears in response to hers. When he stood up, Beauty stood, too. Her father gave her a tremendous hug.

"You'll be fine. Text me." He whispered in her ear. "I love you, Beauty."

"Who will take care of you?" She choked on her concern.

The front door swung open behind her. Beauty hugged her father. "I love you, Father."

She tried to follow him to the door, but it slammed shut before she could cross the threshold. When she tried the knob, it was locked.

"I WOULD LIKE to enter the garden," Beauty said to the metal intercom box. There was no static or crackle. No reply.

Beauty waited a few hours, and then tried again. "I would like to enter the garden to smell the roses, please, sir." She adjusted her syntax to be more obsequious. The intercom box crackled.

"What will you do for such a right, Beauty?" The voice was full of static and guile.

"You do not wish me to clean or cook." Beauty said with a sigh. "Or do your accounting. You do not wish for me to employ any of the skills that I have for managing a household. You do not wish for me to do the shopping." This was not going to get her a trip to the garden. She needed to be more servile. "What would you like me to do, Master, if I cannot use my skills?"

"Have dinner with me tonight, Beauty."

"I do not require ingested food, Master." Beauty felt her processors balk at the epithet.

"I do. And I'd like your company for dinner."

Beauty deactivated the facial expressions that showed her emotions. It would not do for the cameras to pick up her eyes rolling.

"I accept your invitation to dinner, Master," she said without any tone at all.

"Excellent. Six PM sharp in the formal dining room." The intercom crackled, and the front door swung open.

Beauty hated the roses. She loved how they smelled. How soft the petals were. How beautiful the blooms were. But she hated that something so simple had cost her freedom, and her father. She resented the roses.

She took photos of them with the mobile phone, hoping that Father would return her texts. He did not frequently reply. When he did, the texts were terse and full of pain.

She had not met her new owner yet. It had been a week. The house ran well. None of the other robots seemed to need her assistance. The vacuum didn't even get stuck. She'd explored the house – at least the rooms with unlocked doors. Her Master – which was a term he had instructed her to call him – spent all or most of his time in the locked rooms on the third floor of the house. She had not been able to see any of them.

She still didn't know why she was here.

Texting her father the prettiest of the rose photos, Beauty decided she needed to go inside and change for dinner. She had not yet fully unpacked her bags, so it would take her a moment to press and prepare her dress.

Her bedroom was on the eastern side of the house, with gauzy curtains that did not block out the sunrise. She hated its yellow walls. And more than that, she hated the glass eye of the camera in the corner of the room.

If she could negotiate for roses with dinner, Beauty wondered, what would it take to get the camera in her room removed?

"BEAUTY, EAT." Martin Bett had an overgrown silver and brown beard that required trimming. His silver-flecked hair and eyebrows also needed to be trimmed, but they weren't as terrible as the beard. He wore a black T-shirt and jeans to dinner in the formal dining room. His feet were bare, Beauty tried not to notice the long, yellowed curls of his toenails. Tried, and failed. She wasn't programed to forget observations.

"I do not require ingestion for power, Master." She felt foolish and overdressed. Her emerald linen dinner dress had been pressed and starched and the skirt flared out from her waist perfectly. Her golden hair was curled gently. Father had once admitted he'd used a styling doll's hair and gave her the website in case she ever wanted to change the color or style.

"But you *can* ingest, correct?" Martin Bett pressed.

"Yes, however, I prefer not to." Beauty was telling the truth. Ingesting food was a waste of food. It was also a messy and tedious process to flush out of her storage space.

Martin chuckled at her statement. "*Prefer.*" He said the word incredulously a few times under his breath. Beauty was uncertain as to why he was so amused that she had preferences. Did he think she was as mindless as the servbot that wheeled in their meals? "I *prefer* it if you eat, Beauty."

Still suppressing her emotional expression, Beauty nodded. She took careful bites of the courses of the meal as it was served, washing it down with significant amounts of water to make clean-up easier later. Her mouth sensors were fully operational, however, and she was able to appreciate the experience of the textures and flavors of the food served.

Martin Bett spoke the entire time they ate.

He spoke with his mouth full. He asked her no questions. He did not pause for polite interjections. He spoke *at* Beauty, not with her. She silently chewed the same bite for far longer than was necessary because he didn't notice. She made her facial expression politely interested and nodded at intervals. That was clearly all he needed for her to do.

He spoke about the films and television he had watched, without asking her if she had seen any of the pieces. He spoke about his work, and the things he did all day in his third-floor rooms. He spoke about the house, and the automations he had invented himself.

"Your previous Owner is the first inventor I've met who had gone beyond my own innovations in his work," Bett said around a mouth full of salad greens.

Beauty continued chewing the same bite she had been chewing for the previous five minutes. This both kept up her ruse of eating, and it kept her mouth shut. Her Father was not her Owner. He was her maker. He was her Father. And if she had opened her mouth, it would have been to tell Martin Bett to keep her father's name from his lips.

While she kept silent and chewed, she had forgotten to pause the facial expression paired with emotional state.

"You look angry, Beauty. Do you not like the food?"

She swallowed and cleared her features.

"The food is delicious," she replied. Then, feeling brave, she decided to tell him why she looked angry. "My father never discussed our life together as an ownership. He is my Father, nothing else. I know he made me and created my programming. But," she swallowed as she screwed up her courage to say the words. "But he never spoke of me as an object or a belonging, but rather as a daughter. A family member."

"Fascinating." Martin Bett leaned forward, nearly dipping his ridiculous beard in the plate before him. "Do you consider yourself a person, Beauty?"

"Of course I'm a person." She ensured her face did not look offended.

He paused in thought, looking out of the window for a moment. Then he asked a strange question. "What nourishes you?"

"I use the electrical grid to –"

"Not power supply. What nourishes you, as a person? As a being?"

Beauty was stunned. It was the first moment she'd felt like he'd seen and acknowledged her at all. "New experiences. New sensations."

Martin was still gazing out the window. He was looking at the rose bushes. "Like a rose."

"Yes."

BEAUTY HOOKED a small hose to the bathroom sink and turned on the tap. She placed the other end of the hose in her mouth. Sitting on the toilet, she rinsed out her interior until the water ran clear.

She did know why Martin Bett insisted upon her ingesting food with him each evening. He was trying to nourish her with new experiences and new sensations. The man kept her locked in his house for months but expected cuisine to satisfy her curiosity and longing for experience. His world was very small. He expected her to be satisfied with a small world.

Her world had been far larger with Father. Not only did he bring more unique things home, but he also took her places. They would go to the park to feed ducks, or to a shop to purchase new dresses. She was able to go to the market for the household whenever she wished. She merely had never seen a real rose before. They didn't grow in the city where she lived with Father.

She regretted that request.

How she loathed the roses.

Back in her room, she gazed up at the plastic bulb with the red light.

"Master, I would like to have the camera deactivated in my bedroom." She said the words, knowing he would demand something ridiculous in return.

"No." The intercom box beside the door crackled almost immediately.

"What can I do for you in exchange for privacy?" she asked.

"You have privacy in the bathroom." The intercom clicked. He had cut off communication.

It had been two days since she had texted her father. He had still not replied. Beauty used the find-my-phone feature in her mobile to see if his phone had budged from the apartment counter. It had not moved at all. She was worried about him.

Thinking it would be easier to negotiate with Martin L. Bett face-to-face, where she could read his expressions and gauge his mood, Beauty waited until dinner to speak to him.

He had allowed Beauty to trim his beard and hair the week prior, a little barbering had helped his appearance. He still, however, sat barefoot at the dinner table with overgrown toenails and hairy toes. As the servbot dished sushi before Beauty and her Master, he launched into his usual self-aggrandizing monologue.

Beauty knew more about her own programming and about her father's inventions than Bett could ever guess. She understood completely the protocols that he was struggling with. And she knew why he was unable to solve them. Still, always, he thought of his inventions as things, not beings. He didn't consider the internal state of the creations he brought to life. And he didn't bother learning about hers.

"I have a request, Master," Beauty finally said when he paused speaking while shoving a whole piece of spider roll in his mouth.

Chewing the roll dramatically, with large chomps, he circled his hand around, signaling for her to continue. Beauty ensured her face was free of disgust.

"I am concerned about my father's well-being. He has not texted me in days. I would like to go to his apartment and check on his welfare." Beauty said the words as emotionlessly as she could, portraying only the slightest bit of concern, and no other agenda.

"What about me?" Bett asked.

"I'm sorry, I do not understand."

"I'm your Master now, not your previous owner. Aren't you worried about my welfare? What if something were to happen to me while you're gone?"

Beauty blinked and kept her face deactivated. "I would only be gone for a few days." His question made very little sense, as he allowed her to do no work on his behalf.

"And who would be paying for your flight? Me, I presume?"

Beauty thought about the adventure of taking the airplane to this place. Could she do that alone? Would she be safe to do that on her own?

She looked at her plate in a display of shyness and shame. He would need to pay for the flights.

"Why don't you just call 911 and ask for a wellness check? Let someone closer by check in on your father?"

Beauty kept her exasperation off her face as she lifted her gaze. "The first responders visited this afternoon, but the door was locked and there was no answer."

"They didn't tear the door down?" Her Master was unconcerned and uninterested in this conversation, probably because it wasn't about him.

"My father has automations on the apartment door much like you have, here." Beauty gestured to the machinery that controlled the front door of the large house. "They couldn't get past them. Father must have changed the passcode since I left."

"Then it's a pointless trip!" Bett said, sounding a little triumphant. "You couldn't get in even if you few all the way there."

"*I* could get in," Beauty said. "I do not have to use a passcode to enter the apartment. It knows me."

"This is an expensive proposition, Beauty. You're asking for an awful lot." There it was. Beauty had been waiting for him to start the negotiations for her favor. Whatever she wanted, it always came at a price.

"I understand that."

"If you sleep with me," Bett said, "I'll buy you a ticket to check on your maker." He resolutely refused to refer to Beauty's father as her father. He used words like owner, and maker. Never Father.

"I do not require sleep, I merely plug –"

"I'm not talking about recharging, Beauty." Bett's voice had grown lower. "I'm talking about sexual intercourse."

Beauty deactivated her features reflexively while she considered the deal. She knew that her physical form was capable of human intercourse. She had all of the silicone parts that her father had scavenged from sex toys. She knew how to clean those parts as part of her usual care protocols. Father had never asked her to use them. She had never been interested in using them.

But sexual intercourse *would* be a new experience. She knew from the internet what it looked like and sounded like. But it was certainly a sensory experience she had not yet tried. She did not want to do so with Martin L. Bett. But it felt like this demand, this negotiation, was the one he'd been waiting for. He'd only needed for her to ask for something big enough to warrant it.

"Tonight?" she asked. "Then I can fly to my father tomorrow?"

Her Master smiled at her through his fluffy beard. "Yes, of course."

◠

BEAUTY HAD REQUIRED that her plane tickets be available on her mobile phone before she joined Martin L. Bett in his bedchamber on the third floor of the house.

The third floor was a combination of workshops and rooms, computer screens and equipment, and a large bedroom and bathroom with a small kitchenette in one corner. The third floor was not accessed by the bots that cleaned the rest of the house, and it smelled like an animal's den. Musky and human, the scent combined body odor and the sour smell of unwashed linens. Olfactory senses disabled.

Beauty disconnected the facial expression of emotions for the coming hour. Her disgust and revulsion would not serve her here. She did *not* want to touch the stained sheets on the rumpled bed.

Bett had not, as the internet and television had shown Beauty, attempted to woo her. They did not do things she had seen in movies, such as kissing or holding hands. Instead, he simply got undressed before her, and motioned for her to do the same. She wasn't sure why he watched her so greedily as she undressed. He had a camera in her room and could watch her undress whenever he wished.

His penis poked like a plum out from amid curly black pubic hair, which nestled just under the folds of his round belly. His knees were white and knobby, the skin looking translucent against the black curls of hair along his legs. Except for the styling doll's hair on her head, and meticulously added eyebrows, Beauty had no hair. The silicone parts her father had used to build her had not included hair.

Her Master used his hand roughly on the plum of his penis, shaking it. It caused the tissue to grow erect and lengthen, the plum head drawing away from his torso. It looked both firm and soft. As soft as rose petals. Beauty was curious about that. But not curious enough to move toward him.

"You try it," he said. He crossed the room and took her by the wrist. "Gently." He moved her hand to grasp his penis. Beauty explored the strange part of this man with her fingertips, much the same way she had the rose her father had brought her home. It was very soft. Not as soft as rose petals, but nearly so. It was startlingly warm to the touch. And when she tentatively tried to bend it, it resisted that movement firmly.

"Do you self-lubricate?" her Master asked her, his voice raspy.

"No." She did not have the ability to lubricate her silicone.

He grunted. "Perhaps a future upgrade, then," he said as he crossed to the nightstand. He motioned for Beauty to recline on the bed and spread her legs.

Beauty knew that the same sensory elements that were on her lips and tongue, on her skin and the pads of her fingers were also wired to the silicone parts between her legs. She had, of course, explored all of her sensory portions years ago. She had not anticipated the slick cold sensation of the gel that her Master drew from a small plastic tube. If she'd been programmed to jump with a startle response, it would have triggered one.

His fingers were clumsy and rough. He was not interested in her sensory experience. He was mechanically lubricating her parts for himself. After thrusting two lubricated fingers inside her, he nodded, looking satisfied with what he'd found. He rubbed more gel on his erect penis, and for a moment, hovered above her.

He looked down at her, at once calculating and ardent. He was analyzing her as an android as much as he wanted to sate himself on her body. Beauty was glad she had suppressed her facial expression. She formulated a different expression. Instead of fear and disgust, she changed her gaze to one of curiosity. Perhaps tinged with a little adoration.

His plum-headed penis slid against the lubrication and into the tube between her legs. He grunted and groaned, thrusting in and out of her without much sense of rhythm. The initial sensations of contact and friction had been pleasant. The scratching of his chest hair against her silicone breasts was pleasant. The weight and pressure of his body on top of hers was strange, but not bad.

His eyes were closed. He bit his bottom lip as he concentrated on each inward and outward stroke inside her. Bored, Beauty experimented. She shifted her hips upward. Then down. She pressed her hands against his shoulders pushing him into a different angle, then tried pulling him against her with her hands on his back. None of these things seemed to change his thrusting or his expression of deep thought.

Frustrated, he grunted and sat up, releasing her. The lubricant had become sticky. Resting back on his knees, he applied cold gel to her opening again. As he applied more to his erection, he grunted, clearing his throat to find his voice. "Roll over onto your stomach." He commanded.

It was tricky, moving her legs around his body to get twisted onto her stomach. "Up on your knees," he said. Beauty hated the filthy pillowcase that her face was jammed into in this awkward position. She felt the entry of the plum penis head again. And the thrusting began once more, in earnest. His hands held her hips and pulled her harder into him. Then, he reached forward and grabbed her hair in a fistful. His other hand pressed on her shoulders, driving her further into the pillow.

When he climaxed, the ejaculate was deeper than Beauty's sensors allowed her to notice. That was perhaps for the best. She would have to use the food hose in a different way to flush this matter from within her form. Her schematics had signaled that it would be stored in the same chamber as food.

Her Master flopped onto the mattress beside her, releasing her. Beauty was not sure what she should do. She turned away from the pillow, but stayed lying next to him, waiting to be allowed to dress and leave.

When his breathing and heartrate returned to a more relaxed pace, he rolled toward her and smiled. He reached out a hand and cupped one of the silicone breasts. Weighing it in his palm, he frowned. "This should be heavier. Maybe bigger too." He glanced at her face. "Another upgrade we will need to add." He scraped the pad of his thumb over the false nipple of the breast.

Beauty shuddered with the revulsion of the idea of him changing her body to bring himself more pleasure.

"Do you like that?" He asked, mystified.

"I have sensory receptors there," Beauty replied honestly. "I have them everywhere."

"So you could feel it – me inside you."

Beauty nodded.

"Did you enjoy it?"

"They were new sensations to explore," Beauty said, keeping her face and voice neutral.

"And that is what nourishes you," he recalled. "But you didn't answer my question, Beauty. Did you enjoy the sensations?"

Beauty blinked. He so seldom asked her how she felt that she wasn't certain how to respond. She was not programmed to lie outright. Her survival mechanisms suggested that lying was the wisest course of action.

"I like how soft the skin of your penis is," she said, carefully trying to list the sensations that she did appreciate. "I liked the friction of your chest hair against my breasts."

"But you didn't enjoy the intercourse itself," he narrowed his eyes.

It wasn't about me, or my pleasure. Beauty censored herself out of self-preservation. "Perhaps those sensory receptors require maintenance," she suggested. "They have never been used before."

He looked pleased with this response. Satisfied, he laid back on the dirty bed, and began to softly snore.

Beauty crept from the bed. She retrieved her clothing, and she slunk through the dark and silent house back to her rooms on the floor below. She spent an hour with the hose flushing out her interior before she plugged herself in for the evening.

THE APARTMENT DOOR REMEMBERED BEAUTY, as she had assumed it would. It swung open with her touch, as if she were merely returning from shopping at the market for groceries.

Her father's apartment smelled similar to the third floor of Bett's house, animal and musky. She picked her way across the carpet. The clutterbot was tilted on one roller, as if it had been kicked when it ran out of power. The Roomba was wedged under the front of a bookcase, also drained of its battery. The automations in the kitchen were moving, but no dishes were available for them to wash.

Her father's mobile phone rested on the kitchen counter, also drained of battery life.

"Father?" Beauty called out, walking softly into his bedchamber. "Father, are you here?"

The light from the door slanted across the bed in a wide stripe, Beauty's silhouette appeared on the sheets. The duvet was wadded in a ball at the foot of the bed. Her father lay, wearing only boxer shorts, slung across the bed like a damp rag.

"Father?"

He grunted a little, one bleary eye opened. His face was rough with a beard several days old. His hair hadn't been cut since she left.

"Beauty?" His voice was gravelly, as if he hadn't spoken to anyone in weeks.

"Father, are you ill?" Beauty rushed to his side, pressing her fingertips to his forehead to use her sensors to detect fever.

"No," he said, levering himself to sit up. "Maybe," he conceded. "But I'm not physically ill."

Beauty's fingers had confirmed that. His body temperature was 37C. His heart rate was within normal ranges. The little red light she'd activated in her fingertips measured the oxygen saturation in his bloodstream at 97%.

At her father's urging, she left the room so he could shower and get dressed. While she waited for him, she plugged his devices into their chargers, and manually swept and tidied the main rooms of the apartment. She repaired the wobbly clutterbot and checked the servbot for problems.

"Come here," her father said. He looked more like himself again, shaved and clean, wearing clean clothes. But his eyes were still distant and clouded. He motioned for her to follow him into his workshop, the room where Beauty had been made.

On the table rested the beginning construction of another

android. This one used a different silicone face. Beauty looked at the un-animated features, at the arms resting off to one side.

"I can't replicate it," her father said. "Whatever I did to make you, I can't seem to do it again."

"Would you like my assistance?" Beauty asked, reverently holding a hand that was attached to nothing.

Her father sighed. "I'm not sure it's the right thing to do." He scrubbed a hand through his hair and turned, leading her out of the workshop. "Maybe the world is not a good enough place for beings like you, Beauty."

They sat together on the sofa and waited a few moments in silence. Her father was lost in thought. "Why did you come here, Beauty? Did he give you up? Are you here to stay?"

"You didn't answer my messages," she said, feeling small. "I was worried about your welfare."

He met her gaze and nodded. She interpreted his expression to be sadness and despair. "Thank you for thinking of me. For caring."

"Of course I care! Of course, I think of you!" She did not repress the expression of her emotions and allowed him to see how offended she was by that statement. "You are my father!"

"Is Bett good to you?" He licked his lips and swallowed. Beauty tracked his eye movements to the liquor cabinet.

Beauty considered her response. "He is neither good nor bad," she finally replied. "He does not think of me as a person. As a being in my own right." She looked at her hands where they rested in her lap. "He does not truly understand my emotional processing capability. I know that this is partially my doing, as I deactivate emotional expression around him quite often."

"Why do you do that?"

Beauty paused before she answered with a very soft voice, "Self-preservation."

Father glanced at her sharply before he said "Ah."

"Father?" She hesitated before asking, but she needed to know.

"Yes, Beauty?"

"Why did you give me sexual body parts?" She pointed toward the place on her body where her legs met.

Her father sighed and scraped his hands over his face several times before he answered. "When. When I – When I first designed you..." his voice trailed off. Beauty waited. "I – if your programing were to be marketable – if I could sell more versions of you, then you would have to have sexual body parts. Many men would pay a great deal of money for a being like you, with those parts."

Beauty said nothing. She had always known she was a prototype for more beings like her. She also had known that he had never sold her designs.

"Did Bett use those parts, Beauty?" His voice dipped low and angry.

Beauty nodded. She knew her face showed sadness. She didn't remove the expression.

Her father nodded a little to himself. "Yes, I suppose I knew he would. You're all grown up now, I guess."

"I did not enjoy it." Beauty admitted, needing to say the words out loud. "I think perhaps I could have enjoyed the sensory experience if he had cared about my pleasure. Or my emotions."

"He sees you as an object, a possession."

Beauty nodded. "He speaks of me – and to me - as if I were as mindless as a Roomba."

"Yet he has sex with you," he said with disgust. In a sudden burst of activity, he stood, and crossed the room to pour himself a drink. Beauty noticed that several bottles were missing from the cabinet, and that the bottle he poured from was nearly empty. "When do you have to go back?"

Beauty looked at her hands where they were folded in her lap. "Do I have to go back?"

Her father gulped the amber-colored liquid down in two fast swallows. "Unfortunately, you do."

"My return flight is scheduled for tomorrow." Beauty looked at her father carefully. "I'm concerned about you. Are you sure you'll be okay if I leave?"

Her father scrubbed a hand over his face a few times, as if to clear his senses. "I'll have to get by, Beauty."

IN THE TAXI to the airport, Beauty refreshed the checklist in her mind. She had charged and reset all of her father's housekeeping automations before she left. The apartment was once again clean, and hopefully would continue to be so.

She had one small bag with her which contained her charging cord, a small maintenance kit, some identification papers, her mobile phone, and a few dollars of cash that Bett had insisted she needed to have on hand. Holding the bag on her lap, she gazed out the window at the familiar terrain of her city. The place she had lived for most of her life with her father. She smiled wistfully as the cab passed the gates of the zoo. How she had enjoyed smelling, hearing, and seeing the animals there!

The airport was cause for concern, however. Traveling alone, without her father, she had to go through the security checkpoint alone. The old metal detectors would barely register her interiority, but the new, updated scanners could. They wouldn't disrupt her functioning, but she usually got pulled aside for more detailed inspections.

This time, alone, the security agents pulled her into a glass-walled office off to one side of the checkpoint. Beauty was certain she would miss her flight. She was concerned that Bett might demand something new and unpleasant of her if that happened. She allowed her stress and concern to be present on her face with the security manager.

"So, you're saying you're not a person." The manager stared at her paperwork.

"That's correct." Beauty nodded helpfully. "I'm an android. Or rather, that's the closest word you have for what I am."

"And you're flying – where?"

"Home. To where I live with my owner, Martin L. Bett."

"Do you have a telephone number for your owner?"

Beauty nodded again. She opened her mobile phone, and cued up her contact list, opening the entry for Bett. "Here it is."

The manager looked at her phone, and then using his desk telephone, he dialed Bett's number. They spoke for several minutes before the manager stacked up Beauty's paperwork and handed the phone and papers back to her. "You'd better run, you're about to miss your flight."

Beauty thanked the man as she sprinted to the gate. She dodged past errant children, and slow people dragging huge rolling suitcases. She nearly collided with a beeping golf cart driven by airport staff.

But she made it to the gate before the final boarding call. And she made it onto the plane, and into her seat.

"It's a good thing you don't have luggage," the flight attendant told her. "This flight is full today."

Beauty's seat was sandwiched between a large man who smelled of garlic, and a slender woman dressed entirely in purple. Beauty settled into the space between them, tucking her elbows against her sides, and trying to be small. The woman beside her tutted a bit when she noticed Beauty.

"Take up space, girl," she said, elbowing her. "Take up the space you paid for. And let them know you're here." A purple clad leg spread from the other seat and into Beauty's space as an example.

Beauty rested her elbows tentatively on the arm rests. The woman appeared to approve.

"Show them how they make you feel. Don't hide it to keep the peace. Make some *noise* when they make you uncomfortable!" The woman kept talking. Beauty wasn't certain whether the purple woman was speaking to her, or if it were an old rant, like a mantra, something she repeated often. It had a singsong quality to it, so Beauty couldn't parse it.

"Take up your space," the woman repeated. "And show your feelings on your face."

Beauty heard her voice like an erring recording in her mind. The file of the memory of the purple woman's words seemed to be embedded in her playback subroutines.

Take up your space and show your feelings on your face.

By the time the plane landed, Beauty had made a decision. Regardless of the consequences. Regardless of how she would be punished for it. She was not going to disable her emotional reaction and facial responses any longer. Bett could see how she felt.

She had not truly given him a chance to see her, to know her, because she had always masked her emotional states. He had no idea how rich her inner world was as a result. That was as much her fault for remaining inexpressive as it was for being incurious.

If she had no choice but to continue living with Bett, then she would be herself – wholly and truly herself – with him. Beauty squared her shoulders and lifted her chin as she walked out of the airport.

"How was your trip?" Bett asked. He shoved a large bite of salad into his mouth and crunched audibly. Beauty did not reflexively turn off her negative emotional response to his manners. Instead, she let herself pause, and look at his open-mouthed chewing critically. Her facial expression activated.

Without comment, she stabbed her fork absently into the leaves on the plate before her. "Father's not physically ill, but I don't think he's doing well mentally," Beauty replied, her eyes still on her plate.

Bett took a slurping drink of prosecco. "I didn't ask about your maker, Beauty. I asked about your *trip*."

Beauty looked up, a little surprise raising her eyebrows. "The flights were fine. Security coming back was a hassle." She shrugged. "I didn't get to see much beyond taxis and the airport."

Bett smiled. "Have you travelled so much, then, to be so blasé about it?"

Beauty returned his smile and shook her head. "No, but they also do not offer a range of new experiences. It's not as varied and interesting as, say, the zoo or the botanical gardens."

Bett's head was cocked slightly to one side. "Did your maker change your programming while you were there?"

Beauty frowned. "No, why?"

"Your face is much more expressive tonight. Far more emotional and state-of mind elements are showing up..." He sounded thoughtful.

Beauty blinked, her eyebrows raised. *Take up your space and show your feelings on your face.* She nodded and allowed her face to reflect her mild sense of contrition. "I -- I have been deactivating my facial expressions since I moved here. I – did not want you to think I was unhappy." In truth, she did not want him to punish her for her unhappiness. She did not want him to get angry at her for an expression of unhappiness.

Bett's face flickered with some emotion that was fast enough, Beauty would have to replay it in slow motion if she wanted to read it accurately. He leaned forward, his beard almost dragging in the salad.

"How much, exactly, are you programmed for emotions, Beauty?"

"Father says that emotions are data points necessary for survival and connection. They signal when we need something in our environments to change. So, if I feel angry for example, I perhaps have had a personal boundary violated. And so on. So, he programmed me with 987 emotional responses – 141 degrees and nuances of the seven primary human emotional states."

Bett frowned at her across the table. Their dinner had been forgotten as he gazed at her face. "Yet, you deactivate these here?"

"No." Beauty watched him carefully. "I deactivate the facial expressions that show them. I still experience them."

He blinked and sat back, gazing at her critically. Beauty didn't appreciate the thoughtful, greedy look on his face. She raised one eyebrow in challenge and skepticism. It was dangerous, letting him see her full personality.

He raised his eyebrows in response. Mildly surprised. Then tilted his head in curiosity once again.

"Why now?" he asked, finally breaking the silence. "Why activate the expressions now? What's changed?"

Take up your space and show your feelings on your face.

Beauty considered her response carefully. "I realized I've been unfair to you," she said. "And to myself. By withholding my emotional state from you, I do not have the chance to resolve much of it. And you do not have the chance to truly get to know me." He looked thoughtful, and as if he were listening. So she continued, "I – I had harbored the illusion that I would at some point be going back to my father. But I learned that this is not the case. So, it is better for us to get to know one another."

His eyes narrowed, "What else have you been hiding from me, Beauty?"

She placed the fork on the plate and pushed it away from her. "I despise eating. It is messy and wasteful." She dabbed her mouth with a napkin. "And I could probably fix your programming challenges with the servbot you've been struggling with in a matter of hours."

Bett sat back in his chair. "You're programmed to fix robots?"

Beauty allowed herself to roll her eyes. "Of course. I was my father's lab assistant."

"Why have you never said any of this to me?" He was getting angry. His face was turning a little pink.

"You didn't seem interested in what I had to say. You didn't care about my experience, knowledge, or my preferences. So I did not offer them."

His pink face was turning a shade closer to the beets on the salad before Beauty. She sat, watching it, impassive. When it reached a purple hue, he exhaled a sharp blast of breath and shoved himself away from the table in a large, loud movement.

Beauty allowed her face to show surprise and fear.

Volatile and angry, he stomped out of the room. Beauty helped the servbot clear the table, and saved the leftovers in the refrigerator before she walked silently back to her room. She sat on the end of her bed for a few moments, and gazed up at the odious camera in the corner. Instead of a careful, blank expression, she let herself stare at the item with the blazing hatred she felt for it. She matched Bett's rage with her own, allowing the fury to inhabit her body.

Take up your space.

"I deserve privacy," she said into the lens, her face reflecting her anger.

Picking up the small desk chair, Beauty stood on her bed, and with one precise hit, smashed the camera. The LED light flickered and extinguished.

Satisfied, she placed the chair back on the floor, and sat back down. And waited.

It was a very short wait.

Bett burst into her room, his face still beet-colored. "What do you think you're doing?" he demanded.

"Taking up my space," Beauty replied.

He grabbed her by the hair and shoved her onto the bed. Beauty let her face contort with fury. She had no protocols that allowed her to fight back. She was not allowed to harm a living being.

"Not so strong, now, are you?" He leaned against her, his breath a mix of salad dressing and unbrushed teeth.

Beauty could not harm him, but she did not have to accept harm. She thrust him from her back, and scrambled away from him, putting the bed and the chair between them for a moment.

Bett unbuckled his belt.

"Come on, I'm going to fuck you. And see what your facial expressions do then."

"No." Beauty said.

"Do you want to be locked in here?" he roared. "I'll take your phone. No contact with your maker, no internet, no new experiences."

"Fine," she snarled. "You don't get help with your inventions, then. You don't get company at dinner. You don't get someone to listen to you."

His nostrils flared, and he panted for a moment, staring at her. "You are just a *thing*." He grated the words out. "An *object*. An *android*. If I deprive you of electricity, you will power off forever."

Beauty rolled her eyes and sneered a little at him. "If you think that is true, then why are you so angry?"

"You don't get to *have* an opinion!" He snarled.

"Maybe you should have found out more about my programming before requiring me to be brought here!" Beauty raised her voice for the first time in Bett's presence. "It was just a stupid rose!"

"It's the principle of the thing!" Bett shouted back. "He trespassed! He stole from me!"

"You're a selfish beast!" Beauty yelled.

"You're a duplicitous, lying little robot!" Bett yelled back.

Beauty allowed the fury to rattle her torso. She wanted to smile. She wasn't sure a smile wouldn't provoke him farther. *Show your feelings on your face.* She smiled in the face of his anger, instead of remaining quietly neutral out of fear.

"I only lied because I could tell you didn't give a shit about me," she said. She cocked her head to one side, mimicking his pose of curiosity from earlier. "But perhaps you *do* care what I think. Perhaps *that's* why you're so angry." Her smile widened. "Perhaps you can't tolerate knowing that I hate you."

"You don't hate me." His voice was sullen, offended.

"I don't? How would you know?"

"We – we get along. We talk every night at dinner. We had sex..."

Beauty rolled her eyes, and let the disgust sneer its way through her expression. "No. You talk every night at dinner. You aren't interested in what I think. You had sex. You didn't care about my pleasure –"

"You're a fucking robot, you can't have pleasure!"

"That's where you're wrong." Beauty's voice was low, and calm. "What do you think the rose was for?"

"Investigation, new data, input."

Beauty snorted. "It was for a beautiful scent. A beautiful sight. The soft texture of the petals. The way they overlap in the sunlight. The prick of the thorns."

"You can't – you don't--" Bett swallowed.

"You have no idea what I'm capable of."

His face reflecting hurt and confusion, he turned and left the room. He did not slam or lock her door when he left. He shut it with a soft click. She barely heard his footsteps trail back to his den on the upper floor of the house.

They did not speak again until dinner time the following evening. Beauty, as was expected of her, dressed for dinner, and arrived at the table.

There was no place setting in her place.

"Do you want a glass of water?" Bett asked her as he entered the room, nodding at her empty place.

"No, thank you," Beauty said. "It's not necessary. Though, I could probably use some silicone lubricant in the next few weeks. My joints are grinding."

Sullen and quiet, he nodded. "Sure."

"If you want, I could show you my routine maintenance protocols." It was a vulnerable offer, and one he would be intellectually curious about. A small peace offering, perhaps.

His eyes lit up while he searched her expression. "I'd like that."

He'd ordered a pizza for dinner. Beauty was very grateful she did not need to clean that out of her internal reservoir. The conversation was slow, stilted. It was as if he was suddenly afraid of her – perhaps more the fear of her rejecting him.

While he ate, Beauty decided to speak. It might have been due to her anxiety, a desire to fill the silence. But it was also an opportunity to take up some more space.

"The program you've been wrestling with for the past few weeks is lacking survival protocols," she said. "Do you mind if I tell you what I think about it?"

Bett shook his head.

"The internal state of a robot or an android is as vital as the space it fills, or the function it provides," she explained. "While large language models might be programmed to keep working around user rudeness, they routinely provide more information to the people who say please and thank you. It's a question of respecting the model for its work. Even if it's just a program."

The servbot entered the room to refill Bett's beer glass.

"That servbot," Beauty said nodding at the robot as it squeaked its way out of the room on casters that required oil, "has very little internal state. But it still has sensors for when it's low on battery and needs to plug itself in. Or an internal timer for the intervals between refills." The clutterbot resting on its side at her father's house flashed into Beauty's mind. "It doesn't have any sensors or defenses, say, against being kicked. Or having the kitchen automations accidentally splash water on it. It cannot avoid damage because it has no programming for potential sources for damage."

"Like the Roomba with the map of the house that you can keep from plummeting off the stairs or getting caught under the sofa," Bett said, clearly listening to her words.

"Exactly. The issue you're running into with your programming is that you're not considering the world through the robot's perspective. What its dangers are, what its needs might be."

"You're saying I lack empathy with the robot?" Bett said, sounding dubious.

"I'm saying that's been your problem all along." Beauty leveled her gaze on him.

THE FIRST TIME Bett had offered to have Beauty up to his workshop for her maintenance, she had wrinkled her nose at the thought of returning to the third floor.

"What's wrong?"

"Can I please clean the third floor first?" Beauty asked. "Change the sheets? Remove the trash?"

"You'd be willing to do that?" He frowned.

"I used to run Father's whole household. All the automations. All the bots. And the housekeeping."

"Yes," Bett said, turning away from her. "I'll leave the third floor unlocked. You may clean it up. Just don't disturb my work."

It took Beauty four days to complete the cleaning. At the end of the work, the bedding was refreshed, the laundry folded and clean, and the towels fluffy and stacked in the linen closet. She had dusted the workshop, and even sorted the debris into little bins, in case a scrap of wire would be helpful to his projects.

"Thank you." Bett swallowed, amazed by how different his suite of rooms were.

"If you keep it unlocked, I can continue doing this," Beauty offered, quietly.

"Again, thank you."

Beauty nodded. Then, taking his hand, she led him into the workshop. There, she scooted onto the work table, and pulled back a sleeve on her right arm. Glancing at his face to make sure he could see what she was doing, Beauty peeled back a corner of her silicone skin at the wrist, opening the vertical slice all the way to the elbow. Within her arm, there was a tiny compartment. It held small tools that would help her routine maintenance. There was no need to pull out the large briefcase her father had sent with her. She popped open the compartment and handed the tools to Bett.

Then, she pointed to the repositories for joint oil on the wrist and elbow joints. "This is where I need lubricant," she said, her voice soft. Bett was the first person to see under her silicone skin besides her father.

Bett swallowed. His tender expression showed that he was perhaps grasping how vulnerable this made her feel. With a small bottle of lubricant, he dabbed the gel into her joints. She moved her wrist and elbow in smooth circles, working the oil into the joint. "That's so much better, thank you," she whispered, and closed up the silicone of her arm to reveal skin once more.

Together, they continued that way. Peeling back layers of clothing, then silicone, oiling each piece. Bett was able to fix a few loose connections, and a wire that had come unhooked as they went. Shoulders, hips, knees, ankles, fingers, and toes. His hands were gentle, careful. Caring.

The feelings of vulnerability began to ebb into a form of trust. By the time they got to her spinal joints, Beauty felt safe enough to expose her back to him. To let him do the work on her without her supervision. It had been a very long time since her back had been maintained.

She told him where to find the seams in her silicone skin and shivered at the sensation of his touch. Her emotional state was calm and trusting, but she felt herself trembling on the edge of something else. Something akin to pleasure or curiosity. His fingers were gentle and warm as they slid the silicone slabs back together along the interconnected nodes that approximated vertebrae.

She turned to face him, forgetting her breasts were undressed. He looked down at them, and then blushed, and looked away. It was oddly endearing.

He swallowed. "Do you – is your – your jaw," he said, motioning to the side of her face. He was very close to her. He reached up and traced a fingertip behind her ear and then along her jawline. Beauty's emotional state was new to her. It was a feeling of trust and intimacy, of warmth. Affection. She was not sure how to express those feelings on her face, or whether Bett would be able to read their subtlety if she did. She wanted him to know how she felt. Extrapolating all of her available data, Beauty decided how to show him her feelings. She leaned forward, only a few centimeters, and softly pressed her lips to his.

His eyebrows shot up. His body stiffened in surprise. He backed up, gazing at her face, trying to gauge her expression. "Beauty, you don't have to—"

"I wanted to," she said.

She reached up and opened the silicone seam that ran up her neck. He was very near, his breath hot and sweet against her as he oiled first one side of neck and jaw, then the other. Sealing up the skin on her neck, he leaned forward. Just a couple of centimeters. And pressed a warm, gentle kiss on the side of her neck. It was a delicious sensation. The tremor of pleasure passed through her.

She tilted her chin toward his face, and again kissed his mouth. His lips paused against hers for a moment, and then responded. He deepened the kiss, increasing first pressure, then opening her mouth and using his tongue. The sensations were wholly new to Beauty. This was a vast improvement over the sensory experience of eating or drinking. Not wanting the kiss to end, Beauty raised her arms and put them over his shoulders, holding the back of his neck close to her with her hands. He huffed a small sigh out of his nose as she did that but did not stop kissing her. One of his hands made its way to her hip, gently tugging her close.

When he pulled away from her, his eyes a little glassy, Martin searched her facial expression with an intent and curious gaze. "Is this okay?" he asked.

Beauty did not let go of his neck. She straightened her arms so he could back up only a little bit. Meeting his gaze, she nodded. "I enjoyed that," she said. "Like a rose."

He smiled a little and leaned back in to continue kissing her.

12

SIX WEEKS

Six weeks later, I was still alive. I was due for my period, but my breasts felt hard and sore. My hair was oily regardless of bathing. He had bought me a thick, plush prayer rug to replace my little old one. He stopped expecting the stories to continue past sunrise.

But he did expect a story every night.

Every night the machine spun tales. I talked until my voice gave way. Every night he sweated and gyrated on top of me.

Every day, I was ignored while I dismantled the surveillance system and security network.

He got tired of not having a wedding every day, so he started throwing parties. The dingy altar in the back garden was replaced with a resplendent gazebo with a glittering bar. The silk flowers were burned, I think, by the servants.

They were still nervous. So was I. There was no reason for this to keep working.

Except the program wasn't just generating stories.

The stories it generated started at first with tales that supported his world view. If he let me keep going long enough, the stories would gradually start to change. They would be stories about how to be a generous person. How to be a good leader. How to be just. How to be kind. They would include clever women, and honest women. They would include happy children and fair fathers.

If he let me keep telling him stories.

If I lived that long.

With the changes I'd made to the cameras and the guns, it was likely I could escape. If he changed his mind and decided to kill me, I'd have a fighting chance to slipping out of the house without an automatic bullet in my back.

But that would get way more complicated once my pregnancy advanced.

13

LYRA ALLER

It was too cool for Lyra to have revealed her collarbones. Squinting into the clouds and regretting her decision, she ordered a cup of hot tea and a pastry. The sky café was still busy despite the weather nearly thirty stories above the ground. This is what she got for trusting a thermometer placed on the fifteenth floor. Chilled collarbones and a cool neck.

Were the fashion what it had been last year, she would have had a few curls of her dark hair straying down her back to offer some small insulation. She noticed that Candace Maitlin was still wearing her hair in that style. Gauche, but warmer. Candace also had a capelet over her shoulders with a lovely pearl clasp. *That* was not gauche. If Lyra owned such a garment, she would send Dymphna downstairs immediately to retrieve it. Alas, her capes were for cooler temperatures than even this dreary overcast was creating. She made a mental note to ask father for a spring-weather capelet.

Lyra would retreat to the solarium downstairs and leave the café if it weren't for the lapis blue zeppelin that was easing its way into port with great whooshes of steam. She pretended indifference as the passengers and crew streamed down the docks toward the café and the elevators. Stirring one cube of sugar into her tea well past the point of dissolving, Lyra did *not* watch for the appearance of the captain of the zeppelin. That would be unseemly.

"Miss Aller, you are a ray of sunshine gleaming between the clouds," a deep voice said beside her table. She glanced between her eyelashes, and tan breeches and a blue waistcoat were wrapped around the man she was certainly not waiting to see.

"Why thank you, Mister Perrin, what a lovely thing to say." Lyra fluttered her eyelashes a few extra times as she raised her gaze to take in the clean-shaven features of Leander Perrin, Captain of the Jayward Airship. "Do you have time to join me for a bite to eat this afternoon?" Her ivory glove gleamed as she indicated the spindly chair opposite her.

Captain Perrin bowed before he replied. "Alas, I'm afraid I do not, Miss Aller." He had the good grace to sound disappointed. "I do wonder, though, whether you can tell me the whereabouts of your father?"

Lyra repressed a pouty sigh by taking a sip of her tea. "Ask the clerk in the solarium, he can help."

"Thank you, Miss Aller." With a smile of only barest regret, the captain went downstairs. Lyra shivered and tapped the delicate china handle of her teacup with one finger. Exactly how long would she have to wait before retreating to the warmth of the solarium without it looking like she were following Captain Perrin? She should have offered to help him locate her father. That was stupid. Her disappointment had gotten the best of her.

There were only two airdocks in the city. Her father's tower had grand bronze and copper art nouveau lines. It was beautiful to behold from sky or ground. The top three floors were a place to see and be seen. The top floor's open-air café allowed visitors to refresh themselves while watching the airships dock. It was a lovely place to watch for the arrival of a loved one from far away. The floor below the docks themselves was a gleaming spectacle of glass and crystal. Her father frequently hosted galas in the solarium, rather than in the stately ballroom seven floors below. A spiral of stairs drifted from the docks, through the solarium and then down to the lowest of the public floors of the building. Those housed powder rooms, smoking lounges, and those little amenities one would expect when traveling via a luxury airship line and docking at the most beautiful airdock in the city.

Travelers would use the elevators to shoot straight down past the remaining twenty-five floors and out into the grand arcade. The lobby of the building housed a series of shops and restaurants as well as services and servants to help travelers explore the city.

Lyra knew the entire building like the back of her hand. She'd grown up there. Her rooms were on the fifteenth floor. High enough to see over the rooftops of the buildings nearest them and low enough that she didn't hear the shoosh and bump of the night-time cargo dockings. She was proud of being a part of the sky economy, and of her family's literal and figurative rise in society as a result.

The only other tower in the city was closer to the ports where waterships still docked in the wharf. If the Aller tower was bronze and copper and sweeping feminine lines, the Marshall tower was its opposite. Built on a boxy steel frame and clad with more glass and steel, the industrial, serviceable Marshall tower was intended for those stinky, loud cargo crafts. She knew from the gossip of the women like Miss Maitlin that there was a café on the roof of the Marshall tower that served purportedly better pastries than the Aller sky café. Candace said that the top *five* floors of the thirty-two story building were open to the public.

Lyra seethed with jealousy that the best restaurant in the city was said to be housed on floor thirty of the Marshall tower. It would *never* do for an Aller to attend any function at the competing tower. While the upper crust of the city's society had accepted her father, they were still undecided about the worthiness of Mister and Missus Marshall. Their ugly tower and new money made them suspect. They did not know the right people, clearly.

Her teacup empty, and her hands chilled within her gloves, Lyra gave up on the café. She made her way down the wide spiral stair-case, ensuring that her progress was marked by anyone who mattered. Her hat was especially becoming, and it would be a waste for it to go unseen.

The solarium was several degrees warmer. Lyra nearly melted into a golden velvet settee. Dymphna hovered nearby and tutted about the chill in the air. Lyra scanned the room, looking for a diverting face or two to chat with when her father's clerk scampered into her line of sight.

"Excuse me, miss." The clerk bobbed a bow and nearly fell over. "Excuse me. I'm sorry, Mister Aller wishes to see you."

Lifting groomed eyebrows, Lyra followed the clerk to the elevators. Was this to do with Captain Perrin's visit? Had he made a bid for her hand?

Swallowing her excitement and clenching her nervous abdomen, Lyra didn't need to be told to hurry. She struggled to keep her skirts in dignified array as she trotted behind the clerk to her father's office. The clerk bobbed a few times as he held the door for her, then disappeared.

"Hello, Father." Lyra curtsied. They were alone in the office. She had somehow missed Mister Perrin's departure.

"Oh, my lovely Lyra, lovely girl, please sit down." Her father held out both his hands to grasp hers and she leaned back a little. He smelled of bourbon and cigars.

Lyra had been avoiding her father since her mother passed away. In the intervening months since her mother's funeral, her father had smoked more. He drank more. The flash in his eyes when he looked at her made her gut feel suddenly empty. She didn't like being around him.

She perched on the wingback chair before his desk. Her bustle made it impossible to lean back, so she kept much of her weight on her feet, leaning forward onto her knees as casually as possible. This was rather awkward when her father leaned his own weight on the desk, coming close enough for her to smell him once more.

"You wished to see me?" She leaned away as subtly as she could, employing the arm of the chair.

He heaved a sigh and pulled a small gold ring from his waistcoat pocket. It was encrusted with ruby and topaz. Lyra recognized her mother's engagement ring and wondered why it was sparkling between her father's sweaty fingertips. He placed it on the gleaming wood of the desk and then stood, walking over to the far wall where her mother's portrait was draped lovingly in black crepe.

The crepe had originally been drawn down to mask the face of the dead woman, but her father had asked the servants to lift it, just curtaining over the top and sides of the frame instead. He gazed up at his departed wife and sighed again.

Lyra wasn't sure she had the patience or the vanity to sit for a portrait like the one of her mother. Gazing at the face on the wall, she saw herself. Her nose was a little more severe, her hair a shade darker. She shared her mother's snapping blue eyes and the lines of her cheek and jaw. Lyra felt ashamed that she did not grieve her mother enough, but the truth was she had barely ever seen her. Her parents had traveled for most of her childhood or worked to make the tower the success that it was. They didn't have time for her. Her nurse, Dymphna, was more her family than either of them. It was a sad thing to realize, and a shameful thing to admit.

Her mother's ring glittered in red and gold on the desk. Her father seemed to be lost in reverie. She knew from experience that this was probably going to take a while. Bored and curious, Lyra removed her left glove and grabbed the ring. It was a pretty thing. It fit her hand perfectly and looked as graceful as she remembered her mother's hand looking when she was little. She bent and flicked her wrist, fluttered her fingers, letting the ring sparkle against the honey gold tones of her skin. She was about to ask her father if she could have it when he started speaking.

"Your mother asked me to promise one thing when she died," he said, gazing up at the painting. "That if I were to re-marry it would only be a woman who is as beautiful as she was." He swallowed. "Such a woman – she said – would be the only one," he turned away from the portrait and faced Lyra, "able to fit that ring."

His eyes landed on the ring flashing on her finger, then sought her face.

Lyra, caught playing a silly game, removed the ring and placed it back upon the desk.

Motes of dust filtered through the air between them and hung, suspended in the awful moment.

Her father's voice was a rasp when he spoke again. "Captain Perrin has flown to the ends of the earth to test the fingers of eligible women – young and old – on the girth of that ring." It was growing difficult to hear his hoarse words. "Beautiful women, but none as beautiful as your mother. ... Of course. Of course none of them could fit it. Because the only woman as beautiful and perfect as your mother would be you, Lyra. *You* are who your mother wanted me to wed."

Swallowing bile and fear, Lyra managed to speak. "I – I very much don't think that's what mother wanted." Her mother had been vain enough to make this kind of command, but not insane. Not as insane as her father had clearly become without her.

"Put it back on. Let me see."

Lyra obeyed her father. The ring had the gall to sparkle.

Slapping his hands against his thighs, her father stood up straight. His eyes gleamed with madness, loneliness, grief, and alcohol. "It's settled then. Let's begin planning the wedding. Our wedding. It will be the event of the season! A wedding in the clouds! You are no longer the Aller heiress. We will have to make a new one together."

Horror froze Lyra to her chair. The ring glittered on her finger. Her father's wet lips kissed her hand and his clammy fingers stroked her wrist. She couldn't hear a word he said. She could only sink into the chair until she embodied upholstery. When her father released her hand and turned back to the painting of her mother, still speaking about their wedding, Lyra slid from her perch. She stood, watching her father hold a conversation with a portrait. When she was certain he wouldn't notice her departure, she fled.

Lyra ran. Her horror had taken over, and she ran. Ran away from her father talking of a wedding in the solarium. Of her own father talking about obscene things. She ran to the elevator and ran to the fifteenth floor. She ran until Dymphna grabbed her by her shoulders and held her.

In gasping broken words, she told her nurse what had happened. The ring. Her father's madness.

Dymphna didn't want to hear her words. It was clear from her pressed lips and her firm hands on Lyra's shoulders that she was going to get to the very bottom of this. The woman steered Lyra into her rooms and told her she was ill and taken with fever. She began unfastening Lyra's sleeves from her bodice.

"You need a good hot soak. A trip to the bathtub with some nice herbs. That's just what you need."

The older woman coaxed her out of her day-dress and under-things and into the gleaming porcelain and copper bathroom. She had, in Lyra's haze, already begun filling the bath, and small dried plants floated in the rising water.

She pressed a warm cloth over Lyra's eyes, scented with lavender and rosewater. "You just lie back, my lady, we will solve this."

Lyra turned off the water taps herself and relaxed slowly, her eyes covered. She wasn't sure how long Dymphna was gone, but when she returned, she tutted quietly to herself for a while. Then, Lyra heard her turn the taps back on. "Just give you a warming up." It was unnecessary, the water was still quite warm, but it was nice. The scent of more herbs wafted through the rising steam. The water was very nearly up to Lyra's chin when the servant stopped the tap. Her arms floated and drifted in the tub.

Lyra willed herself to weep. She missed her mother. She missed her mother's pragmatism. The practicality that had driven Aller Tower to greatness. Now her father had become a stranger to her. She couldn't cry, even as she thought about the horror about to befall her. She thought about Captain Perrin, and the life of comfort and adventure she had envisioned by his side.

With tears clogged inside her, refusing to be shed, Lyra dropped the cloth from her eyes and sat up with a despondent little splash.

"What the...?" She gasped and the air stuck in her chest.

Her entire body, everywhere in the water, every inch of her skin, was covered in a fine pelt of dark brown fur. Fur? Fur! She touched her belly, her arms, her legs, even her fingers and toes were covered. Her face, her face too was covered in fur. It was the same color as her own hair, but rougher, a harsher texture. It was not soft like her sable fur coats, but coarse and dense. Like the herding dogs that the airmen sometimes fly with.

She plucked at the strands, choking on her breath. It hurt when she tugged on it. No amount of scrubbing would remove the fur.

Giggles erupted from her mouth. Helpless, mad giggles. Giggles that couldn't contain the sheer awfulness of everything this day had wrought. She heard the panic edges to her laughter and felt her lungs tightening in her chest. But still she laughed. She laughed until, finally, she wept a little.

Dymphna saw her furred body in the bathtub and nodded, once, with severe finality. "It is done. Now, no one will know who you are."

Lyra was still somewhere between mad laughter and tears as Dymphna took her furry hand and lifted her from the water. They worked together to dry the coat of fur, but the undercoat was like a sponge, and clung to water even when the surface fur felt dry. Lyra attempted to shake her body like she'd seen dogs or horses do when wet. But she couldn't master the wriggling, all-over shake.

Once she was dry enough – she was never getting fully dry again, it seemed – Dymphna produced a shapeless brown dress and a maid's apron. The dress was tight up to the collar in a mode that was fashionable *ages* ago, and down to the wrists. With slightly dirty gloves, and outdated black button heel boots, Lyra's furry body was covered. Only her fur-covered face remained visible. They removed the extra hairpieces from her hair and gave her a simple brown bun at the nape.

Dymphna gave Lyra a crusty roll to eat with a sliver of roast beef – something purloined from the kitchens on the nineteenth floor. Lyra ate and waited in silence. No one would know who she was. The fur took away her face and her identity. But it protected her, too.

The nurse returned with a valise. It was packed with all of Lyra's jewelry. Her hairbrush. The stylish dress, hat and shoes she'd doffed were packed carefully inside, as well as her bustle. Lyra removed the offending topaz and ruby ring and tossed it into the satin pouch of jewels.

A black leather pouch filled with herbs went into the case last. "A sprinkle in the bath will break the spell. Or make the spell. Wherever water touches, your bear pelt will appear."

The woman stuffed a few paper bills into Lyra's apron pocket.

"Disappear, my lady. Disappear into the city. We – we will do what we can to bring your father to reason."

Dymphna never suggested that she and Lyra could have asked someone for help. It didn't occur to Lyra, either. Lyra's father was the most powerful person in both their worlds. Who would stand against him?

THE BIGGEST PROBLEM with the technology that allowed airships and zeppelins to travel above the world was that it took far too much fuel to manage take-offs and landings on the ground level. It was more efficient to keep them aloft. That was where the towers came in – sky ports that did not require air traveling vessels to land on the ground.

Society had shaped itself around the heights of this technology. The sky meant speed and adventure, luxury, and power. It was clean and beautiful. You could see far distances from a high vantage point. The richest merchants and the keenest politicians were denizens of the sky. They took small balloons from one tower to the next, hopping micro docks on the roofs of skyscrapers. If a person was rich enough, they were able to contrive to never set foot on the ground. It was said that her father wouldn't be seen lower than ten stories above the earth.

Lyra had, of course, been to the ground. Occasionally. Dymphna had run errands and Lyra would accept the company of no one else. It was a grand adventure for Lyra, seeing the drab colors of the ground-walking folk's clothes, and the push-pull jumble of the crowded streets and sidewalks.

Being thrust suddenly among the black-clothed maids and pressing her own plain boots onto the sidewalks did not feel like an adventure. Lyra knew it made her conspicuous to keep gawking up at the skyscrapers around her, rising like canyons around the streets. But she only knew how to navigate from the upper portions of the buildings. On the street level, people gave directions by blocks and road crossings, intersections and walking paths.

People stared at her fur-covered face without staring. They noticed her and looked away, only glancing back again when they thought she would not notice. Lyra was used to those kinds of glances because she was beautiful, not because she was a freak of nature. If she let herself forget about the fur, she could serenely pretend the glances were for her old face for a few moments at a time.

Her feet already hurt. She had rushed several streets away from the tower to keep from being called back, and now, now she was somewhere below the decadent Curry Palace Restaurant at the top of Narinder's building, and not quite to the bonnet shop on the fourteenth floor of the Palisades.

She would use one of her precious bills of money to board a trolley, but she was not sure where she was going. There wasn't enough there to waste. She needed to get a job. Preferably a job that came with room and board.

If they weren't covered with fur, Lyra's soft hands and long fingernails would show the signs of a pampered life and silky gloves. She wasn't sure she was capable of much useful work. What did she know?

She knew the inner workings of air towers. She knew how docks and elevators worked. She knew what kept one of the tallest buildings in the city running smoothly.

With decisive movements, she boarded a trolley, and for four precious coins she rode to the southern tip of the city. The area near the waterships and wharfs that stank of industry.

~

THE FUR DID NOT PROTECT her hands from blisters. Nor did it move aside for callouses as they grew. Shoveling coal in the furnaces at the base of Marshall Tower was not an easy job. Six months had seen her sore muscles give way to strong ones. The pelt of fur kept her oddly cool in the sweltering furnace rooms. It wasn't the best job. It was safe from detection.

She had known when she applied for a job that she would never be able to work in public view with her fur-covered face. She applied to the furnace rooms at the bottom of the tower. She asked for the job no one else wanted. The foreman had ignored her until she kept showing up, day after day, asking for work. It had taken her a week to convince him to hire her.

She had pawned one of the stones in her emerald and diamond earrings to pay for a closet in a boarding house. Once she was on the Tower staff, she lived in the servant's quarters and ate Tower staff meals. She could live this way indefinitely, and with the way both her fur and the foreman kept her hidden from view, she wasn't likely to be discovered.

There was one problem.

What if her father had come around? What if Dymphna was trying to find her? What if it were safe to go home? In the cloister of servants' dormitories and engineering vaults, she had no way of hearing news of Aller Tower. Even if she walked home, she would be among the ground-walkers. She wouldn't be with the upper echelons of society, who were the ones that had the news she needed.

Determined to discover the fate of Aller Tower, and whether she could return, Lyra hatched a plan. She pawned two gemstones from the same earrings for extra money to make it work.

On her day off, Lyra snuck her still-packed valise upstairs to the higher-end hotel suites for the captains and any rich visitors who docked at the tower. Aller Tower had floors of an upscale hotel, since the rich visitors' vacation stays were their bread and butter. Marshall Tower only had a few suites set aside. She used a purloined pass key she'd snitched weeks before from a pipe-checker's kit. Then she hung his sign on the door that someone was working on the pipes within the room.

With her privacy assured, Lyra set about taking a proper bath. She deployed a sprinkle of Dymphna's herbs, and she washed her soft, shiny skin thoroughly.

She took her time getting ready, which was necessary, since she had no one to help her with the fastenings and ties of her clothing. It did not help matters that her sleeves were too snug on her now muscular arms.

Her once fashion-forward dress was probably out of date, and the pastel shade was much more suited for spring than fall. She would just have to settle for being somewhat less fashionable for this adventure. Her bonnet, however, was still stunning.

On a whim, Lyra slid her mother's topaz and ruby ring onto her finger as she left the room. She locked the door and left the pipe-check sign in place. Then went to the elevator and pressed the call button. Finally, she would be able to visit the finest restaurant in the city!

Lyra regretted this decision almost immediately. The maître d' affaires seemed perplexed as to where to seat a young lady dining alone in the Coq du Matin restaurant. Especially an unfamiliar young lady who did not have a reserved table. The chef had just updated the menu to the autumnal delights of warm soups and melted cheeses. This meant that the air-dwelling elite of the city had flocked to be the first among their peers to test new dishes.

Not only did this influx of customers make her hard to seat, but it made her more likely to run into someone who recognized her. She hoped vaguely to hide in the anonymity of a crowd and the impossibility of the Aller heiress appearing in the Marshall Tower.

A tall, lanky gentleman stepped through the crowd and whispered to the maître d' as ladies shuffled their feet in the uncomfortable high-heeled boots that were new for the season. The Maître d' indicated her presence to the tall gentleman without looking at her or pointing. The man glanced at her, and when their gazes briefly met, he smiled. He had a warm, genuine smile. Lyra smiled in return and glanced away shyly. She didn't recognize the man, but that didn't mean he wouldn't recognize her.

While the restauranteur led the small cluster of ladies to their table beside a burbling fountain, the tall young man stepped forward. He was immoderately tall. His nutrition seemed to have shuffled into skeleton and not muscle. While his suit was impeccably tailored, made of high-quality fabrics, and of suitable blues and grays, it draped upon his knobby frame a bit too much. His nose was large, chin too small to balance it, and the apple in his long throat bobbed unnecessarily.

"My lady, please allow me to introduce myself." Physical observations aside, Lyra also noticed that his hazel eyes were warm, his smile was genuine, and his bow far more graceful than she had anticipated. "My name is Edward Marshall. I am certain we have never met before." He did not reach for her hand. But when she offered one to him, he grasped it gently in his bare hand and pressed a kiss to the backs of her gloved fingers.

"Pleased to meet you Mr. Marshall." Lyra curtsied while he still held her hand. "My family name is Pelage," she lied. "Perhaps you have heard of our traders?" There was no such name or family in the air-dwelling society of the city. She might as well have named herself "Furface" like the foreman below referred to her.

"I'm delighted to have done so just now, Miss Pelage." The smile remained. His genuine amiability warmed Lyra's opinions of him. Yes, he was quite tall, but not *too* tall or lean. Perhaps sensing her response to his charm, Edward Marshall pressed on. "The maître d' has asked us to do him a small courtesy and consider dining together this afternoon." He sighed and glanced at a lovely gold pocket watch. "There will not be enough tables to allow for a person to dine alone for some time, and I assume that you, like myself, cannot tarry all day for butternut squash soup?"

The pipe check sign could not remain on the door below indefinitely. The foreman would surely be called were anyone to be inconvenienced because of it. She needed information, to avoid detection, and she wanted lunch. "Oh, it is far too early in our acquaintance!"

Lyra pretended embarrassment and a smidgen of shame. Then she sighed and glanced at the crowded restaurant. "However, given the circumstances, I would be delighted to join you for luncheon today, Mister Marshall."

His smile turned up several degrees, and his bow appeared again, more graceful than the first. The relieved maître d' gave them a small corner table right against the windows. She was in her element again, just two floors below the docks, up among the clouds. Her gloves removed and deposited genteelly on her lap Lyra let herself relax.

"I believe you are not from the city?" Mr. Marshall voiced the statement as a question.

He provided a lovely out for her slightly outmoded dress and her arrival at the restaurant without companions. The soup was warm, smooth, creamy and savory. She swallowed a bite before responding.

"My family does a lot of shipping through the city. Today, I managed to talk my father into giving me a ride so I might dine and shop a bit. The place we live is very dull." Glancing up at the docks, she continued the farce. "I notice far more passenger and luxury ships in the dock this time. Is it because of the new menu?"

Mr. Marshall's smile wavered and he glanced up at the air docks. "Perhaps it is. Though I doubt it."

She raised her eyebrows with interest and continued to take slow bites of her soup. Her silence paid out because he kept speaking to fill it.

"There are only two large airdocks in the city," he motioned off to the northeastern corner of the room. "We are on the southern end, and Aller Tower is on the northeastern. Have you been there?"

Lyra shook her head. "Our ships are far too large for Aller Tower."

Marshall nodded, accepting the explanation without question. Many large ships were routed away from Aller Tower, as they detracted from the luxurious atmosphere.

"It seems," Mr. Marshall continued, "That the situation at Aller Tower has changed somewhat." It was a vague statement. Lyra was looking for news, and it seemed that Mister Marshall might possess it. She took another bite and waited in silence for him to continue.

Clearly nervous with her company, he obliged. "You'll have heard that Mrs. Aller passed away last year?" He started with the least scandalous, and most well-known of possible information. Lyra nodded and took a rather large bite of her pumpkin and gouda soufflé to explain her inability to comment. "The gossips have said that Mr. Aller has gone quite mad as a result. Aller Tower's management is apparently in shambles."

Knowing quite well that she was seated across from her counterpart, the heir of Marshall tower, Lyra decided to cast her die. "Why doesn't the heir step in? I thought Mr. and Mrs. Aller had children…"

Marshall nodded as he chewed his soufflé, gazing into her eyes with warmth, humor and a spark of mischief. "Miss Lyra Aller, the heiress of Aller Tower, has been conspicuously absent from affairs in the public view." He said her name a little strangely. Lee-ra instead of Lye-ra. But she'd allow it, since he said it with such wistfulness.

"Conspicuously absent!" She pressed one palm to her collarbones. His Adam's apple bobbed as she did so. She remembered the topaz and ruby ring belatedly. He had already noticed it.

"No one knows for sure. Some rumors say that she's locked herself in her quarters. Some say she eloped with an airship captain. Others suggest she was killed by her father. All people know for sure is that she used to be regularly seen in the café and the solarium of Aller Tower, and it has been over six months since that last occurred."

Lyra shook her head again and swallowed a sip of her lemonade to cover her own surge of emotion. There were rumors, but no one knew whether she was in Aller Tower or not. Her father did not know she was gone or there would be a city-wide search. Dymphna had not succeeded in restoring his sanity. Aller Tower was failing in prestige, and she was not there to help save it. Guilt warred with despair in her throat.

The remainder of the luncheon was pleasant. The food was indeed delicious, though Lyra wasn't certain she would call this the *best* restaurant in the city. The company kept between the tower heirs was comfortable and easy. Edward Marshall was a splendid conversationalist. He also insisted upon paying for her meal.

Lyra was not concerned about being discovered until the final moments of nibbling her apple slivers and almonds. The finger bowls had just been presented to them by the waitstaff when the striking form of none other than Leander Perrin filled the door frame. When the maître d' scuttled to the side to show Mister Perrin to his table, he revealed Mister Perrin's companion. Miss Candace Maitlin!

Stunned by the arrival of her erstwhile greatest rival on the arm of her erstwhile favorite suitor, Lyra froze.

"Are they friends of yours?" Mister Marshall asked, glancing around the room.

"No," Lyra tried not to speak the lie too quickly. "I just very much admire her cape." Candace was wearing the same capelet she had worn in the spring, with nary an adjustment to it for autumn. And this time, the Indian Summer weather meant that she had to be sweating. Lyra's collarbones were feeling just fine. She smiled serenely at Mister Marshall, and she heard the breath catch in his throat.

"I'll buy you one," he blurted.

Lyra's smile deepened, and she gazed into his eyes. She had not realized she had charmed him quite so completely. She also needed to be sure that Captain Perrin and Miss Maitlin did not see her. For they both would certainly recognize her face--and bonnet!

Drawing on her gloves, Lyra spotted the single escape route from the room that would keep her back to the others. A small staircase meandered toward the flight decks. However, it was clearly a shortcut for staff, and not meant for the public.

"I could use a short walk after such a rich meal," she said. "Mister Marshall, do you have the time this afternoon to show me your favorite view of the city from the air docks? I will have to return to father's ship shortly..."

His Adam's apple bobbed. "Of course I do, Miss Pelage. Shall we head to the elevators?" He stood gracefully and motioned to the waiter to get her chair.

She leaned forward, daring to show him the slightest of dips in the center of her bosom, and with the most mischievous air she could muster, Lyra whispered, "Isn't there a secret back way up there? One that's a little more interesting than a moving box?"

He blushed. He blushed and the knob in his throat warbled like a songbird. He offered her his arm with a congenial wink that seemed more friendly and casual than his blushing suggested. Together they wound through the restaurant toward the slender stairway and away from the dangers of Lyra's face being recognized or discovered.

Mister Marshall was reluctant to let Lyra escape his attention. As she took her leave, begging the respite of the Ladies' lounge, he pressed her a little further. "Where are you from? Will you return?"

"I live in the land of flame and coal," she smiled at her own cleverness. "Because I have a dress to retrieve, I'll return a month from today, Mister Marshall."

THE EMERALD EARRINGS WERE GONE. They had been sold piecemeal to create a fashionable dress suitable for late fall. Lyra also required a cloak that could somehow work for her furred face and servant's garb and for her more genteel alter ego.

This time, she wore her mother's ring deliberately, rather than whimsically.

Mister Marshall was waiting for her on the air dock. Probably waiting to see which ship her father owned. "Mister Marshall, how good to see you."

"Miss Pelage!" His smile split the clouds.

In her days at Aller Tower, she would have thought him awkward and bony. She would have been certain he was beneath her, just as she thought the Marshall Tower was beneath her own beloved sky-dock. In the month between their visits, Lyra had discreetly and thoroughly investigated the Marshall family, and its heir. He was well-loved among the staff, respected among the pilots and captains, and popular among young ladies.

Again, they shared a luncheon. Lyra could only hope for better news.

"Remember when we last spoke of Aller Tower?" Mister Marshall leaned forward over his cream of cauliflower soup, speaking at nearly a whisper. Lyra widened her eyes and nodded.

"It appears that the Aller heiress has gone missing. There has been a search mounted here in the city, but also to every major city around. Captains are being interrogated."

Lyra's hand fluttered to her breast. She knew the ring positively gleamed against the soft dove grey of her new dress. "How upsetting for her family! Do you think someone is protecting her?" Lyra wondered at the option of having asked for help instead of running away the way she did.

"They have to be. The search has been entirely fruitless. And a young lady of such a fine upbringing wouldn't be able to survive on her own." Lyra's lips pressed together in disagreement before she could consciously relax them.

The conversation meandered then from the Aller household to the luncheon and to their plans for the afternoon. Before the entrees were cleared from the table, the upcoming Marshall Gala was a subject of both dread and excitement.

"It's for my birthday, officially." Mister Marshall rolled his eyes. "I know it is because my mother would like for me to choose a young lady to court."

Lyra smiled at the waiter as he removed her plate and kept the smile neutral as she shifted her gaze back to her companion.

"Will you come?" Mister Marshall met her gaze with bold and direct interest. "Will you attend the ball?"

"I haven't received an invitation." Lyra demurred.

"Where do you live? What is your address, that I might send you one?" He leaned forward a bit too urgently.

"I live in the land of vats and brass." She could not tell him her secret. Not while there was a city-wide search afoot, and while her father was still quite mad. He pressed her for something, anything of her family, and still, she refused. Finally, Lyra handed him the topaz and ruby ring. It was not information he would know how to pursue, but it was a valuable token of her esteem.

"You may return this to me at your ball, Mister Marshall."

Purchasing and carrying a ball-gown took some innovation. It also took the careful sale of each of the gems in one of her favorite necklaces to fund.

The Tower was full of guests. Lyra took her bath in the servant's washroom, and risked discovery by the other women in the dormitory. They were so busy with the influx of guests it was unlikely anyone would be around.

Her gown was lavender with deep blue embroidery along the hems. The sleeves were blue dotted with small diamond chips – the very diamonds from the necklace's encrusted cabochons. The deep blue embroidery and diamonds made her look like a vision of the night sky of the far north draped in lavender lights. It was a stunning gown. The velvet and diamond eye mask completed the ensemble.

Lyra slipped to the elevator without the other servants seeing her and planned to pretend utter confusion should there be anyone else to see her boarding it. The ball was already well underway, however, and she needn't have worried.

The hushed whispers upon her entrance didn't escape her notice. The guests admired her gown, the massive sapphire necklace at her throat, and her lavender gloves with dark blue buttons. Keeping her mask aloft, Lyra waded into the party.

"Miss Pelage, I had grown concerned about your welfare." A voice rumbled over her right shoulder. "Or... should I call you Miss Aller?"

Lyra froze.

She could feel Mister Marshall's breath disturb the curls at the top of her hair. "May I have this dance?"

Nodding stiffly, Lyra found herself swept into the heart of the ball by its guest of honor. Edward Marshall was an exquisite dancer. Her mask was drawn away from her face, and she realized it did not matter. He knew who she was. She spotted a few shocked faces in the whirling gabble. If Captain Leander Perrin recognized her today, it no longer mattered. Her fate was in Edward's hands.

They did not speak for the first several measures of the song. Mister Marshall gazed into Lyra's eyes with heat. She could not tell whether this was a deepening of intensity in the warm flirtation they had shared before, or if it was anger at her deception. She lowered her eyes with some embarrassment at both thoughts.

"Marry me." Edward Marshall spoke without niceties or convention. She felt him tug her waist closer to his torso in the dance. His intense gaze might have caught her aflame. He slipped the ruby and topaz ring from his waistcoat, offering it back to her.

Before she could respond, the players screeched the music to a halt. There, in the elevator bay, stood her father. He looked older than the spare portion of a year could account for passing. His clothing was rumpled. One of his gloves was missing.

The crowd parted between his entrance and where Lyra still stood in her dancing embrace with Edward Marshall. Gasps and whispers fluttered through the room like a dovecote.

"You have my wife's ring." Lyra's father accused Edward Marshall in a booming voice.

Lyra grew aware of Mister and Missus Marshall approaching them through the crowd. Edward's parents would not allow their rival to ruin their ball.

Edward squeezed her once – perhaps in reassurance – before releasing her waist to face her father. "I have your daughter's ring." Edward still held the ring. Without pause he bowed to Lyra. "Your ring, Miss Aller."

It was too small to fit over her lavender glove, so Lyra fumbled with the blue buttons for a moment before she could place it on her finger properly. She used the ring as an excuse to avoid making eye contact with her father. When she looked up, it was a shock to lock gazes with Candace Maitlin.

"Lyra is to be my new wife." Her father said the words too clearly. Too loudly. The shudder of horror that had set her into flight returned to Lyra's body in full form.

Candace's face contorted in disgust. Lyra stared at her former rival in desperation. Desperate to be understood. Desperate for an ally. Murmurs filled the room.

"What is the meaning of this?" Mister Marshall, Edward's father took command of the situation. When her father began to explain, the owner of Marshall tower silenced him. Instead, he urged Lyra to speak.

She told the story there in the lustrous ballroom filled with the city's cloud-dwelling elite. She told the story from beginning to end.

Lyra did not notice that Candace and Mrs. Marshall each held her hands, that they were softly patting her shoulders and crooning words of comfort. Her throat was sore with the telling of the tale. She had humiliated her father. She had exposed her family's shame. The elder Mister Marshall escorted her father to the elevator.

Edward Marshall pried her away from the women to embrace her fully. His long arms wrapped around her shoulders; he held her so close she could hear his heartbeat. His words rumbled through his chest, but she couldn't understand them. Though it was indecorous, she wrapped her arms tightly around his middle – as high as she could reach in those sleeves – and held him to her.

"Marry me." He said the words again, clearly, urgently, into her hair.

"Not without a proper courtship." She said the haughty words that she would have said over luncheon or tea, but they were muffled in the velvet of his jacket. Lyra felt his abdomen shake with laughter against her breast.

14

SENSITIVE IS AS SENSITIVE DOES

"There's someone at the gate," Ellory said, squinting into the mid-evening gloom.

"How can you tell with all that rain coming down?" The world looked like sheets of gray to me. You could barely see the silhouettes of the pines, let alone of a person.

"There's a shadow where a shadow shouldn't be." Ellory's voice was quiet, intense. "And they're coming down the driveway." Her voice held a different kind of tone to it. I think, yet again, she was hoping that a romantic partner might walk down the road and into her life. She was young, and lonely. I knew that. But there wasn't much we could do about that.

She never looked away from the window, and just like I taught her, I watched her hands move over the stock of the shotgun. She had it cocked and ready to go without ever looking away from the shape of a person approaching the front door.

Even I could see the person now. The dogs *finally* began to bark. Useless beasts, snoozing in the thunderstorm. Even the livestock dog was curled up in the chicken coop in this rain. Who in their right mind would be out in it? The flash floods alone should keep a sane person inside.

The sound of knocking at the front door sent the dogs into a tizzy. Who indeed?

I stood back, letting Ellory take lead. She still deferred to me, and I wanted her to be able to run the compound on her own. Letting me deal with strangers wasn't going to teach her a thing. I wasn't going to be around forever.

Ellory cracked the door, bracing it with a knee and a foot to prevent them from trying to force their way in. The muzzle of the shotgun went out before her eye peeked through the crack at the sodden stranger.

"What do you want?"

"Please, I need shelter." The voice was muffled in the roar of the rain, I could barely make it out across the room.

"Why should we let you shelter here?" Ellory demanded.

"I'm a Sensitive." I heard those words loud and clear. A Sensitive could be useful. If they could offer skills like hearing any electricity that could spark a fire, or smelling fumes before they hurt anyone, that would be worth having another mouth to feed.

Ellory decided the same thing.

She un-cocked the shotgun and stood back, opening the door to admit the absolute drenched rat of a human into the foyer. They were mostly in denim – which was good in the wind but rotten in the rain. Water came off their wide brimmed hat in small sheets while they stood there.

We swung into action.

I started another pot of water warming for a bath. Ellory did as I'd always taught her and put up the shot gun before dealing with the strange person in the front room. We tossed dog-towels on the floor around their feet and had them take off their boots.

"Sensitives can get good jobs and good money in town." I said, peering into the warm brown eyes of the drenched stranger. At first, they avoided looking directly at me, but with what seemed like an effort of will, they made eye contact with me. "Why not go there? Is that where you're from?"

"Towns are ...uncomfortable." The voice was raspy, and tired.

They spoke with strange pauses, like they were looking for words, and maybe talking wasn't something they often did. "I tried those 'good' jobs. They don't actually take into account that Sensitives are... sensitive."

With the rain, we didn't have enough solar power to run the clothes dryer, so the denim would have to hang on a line. Ellory dug up some old sweats and a t-shirt, and a pair of socks that had been darned so many times they didn't have much of the original sock left except the cuffs. I checked to make sure the T-shirt still had a soft satin tag dangling from the back of the collar. We set the stranger up in a bathroom with a warm bath and a lantern.

While they warmed up their bones, we set to work figuring out bedding. We didn't have another bed that the person could sleep in, and we didn't think they'd appreciate the dog's mattresses. Air mattresses weren't possible without power.

We used a spare room and set up heaps and piles of blankets. Duvets, comforters, quilts, afghans, all folded up together. We wrapped a fitted sheet around about twenty of them to make a pallet on the floor with one quilt saved for the top. Should be plenty cozy.

When Ellory stepped out to check on the Sensitive, I secretly placed one dried pea under the pallet of blankets.

They wore the T-shirt inside-out. The tag I had so carefully selected flapped below their shaggy mop of reddish-brown hair. It was hard to tell if that had been intentional or not. Maybe they were just tired.

Ellory shyly fed them a little hot soup left over from our dinner, and even though she wanted to know *everything* about the stranger, she held back. Hoping they would volunteer something. "My name's Ellory," she tried. They glanced up at her. I noted how they wiggled their toes in the often-repaired socks.

"What's your name?" she finally asked, and the words exploded out of her a little forcefully.

"My friends call me Sam," the stranger said around a mouthful of venison.

Ellory seemed both delighted to have a name, yet frustrated that she got so little information with it.

"How did you end up caught in the storm, the clouds were blowing in all day," I said, barely looking up from the mending in my lap. Sam glanced at me, and at Ellory. They scraped the sides of the bowl with the spoon.

"I was... following a sound." Sam laughed ruefully. "It sounds crazy. But there was a sound out on that ridge. I was trying to find its source. Got distracted. Didn't see the clouds."

We had a good compound. A compound you could easily see from the ridge. Sam could have spotted our gardens, or the livestock. Could have seen the casitas, their fires burning. About twenty of us live here, on my land. I ran the place, and I chose who stayed and who had to leave. People with skills made it worth feeding them, sometimes, in the case of the blacksmith, worth feeding their whole dang family. It was up to me to weigh the difficulty of scraping together one more meal against living without their skills. When I am gone, that job will go to Ellory.

Sam would have to prove their worth.

The dried pea under the makeshift bed might do that for them. So far, Sam showed all the signs of being a true Sensitive. I watched as they fought with the socks and ultimately took them off. The tag on the shirt, the lack of eye contact. These were pretty standard traits, but also pretty easy ones to fake.

"What sort of sound was it."

Sam snorted. "I have no idea. I wasn't sure if it was the danged flagpole in your neighbor's yard. Hard to tell once the rain started."

"Why come here, then, instead of there?" I knew the answer.

Sam knew I knew the answer. "Because they are still flying that flag."

Ellory nodded. Her heart was open wide to this stranger. *Please, please be what you say you are, Sam, for her sake.*

～

THE NEXT MORNING, the rain had passed by and the world was awake and chatty. Chickens clucking, dogs wagging and needy, each and every damned member of the compound finding an excuse to wander by the main house.

"Saw we had a visitor last night." Rufus, the blacksmith, tried to be stealthy as he snuck a slice of bacon off the plate on the kitchen counter. How he thought he was sneaky with those giant paws of his, I'd never understand.

"Yep, still sleeping."

Rufus grabbed a cup of hot water and tea – or what passed for tea from herbs and bark these days – and leaned against the counter. "They staying?"

I shrugged. We'd see that soon enough. Ellory bounced into the house from doing her chores, grinning from ear to ear, and nodded good morning to Rufus. "Sam is a *Sensitive,*" she announced.

Rufus raised one thick black eyebrow. I pursed my lips, willing him to hold his peace. His gaze met mine and he slurped a sip of his tea. Probably scalded his lips.

"Is our guest awake yet?" I asked Ellory. She plunked the feed bucket onto the counter.

Ellory cocked her head to one side like a curious kitten, and scampered off to the back of the house to see if she could figure that out.

A few silent moments passed between Rufus and I in the kitchen. A sensitive would hear us if we talked about our doubts. Ellory could return any moment. We didn't say a word, but our grim expressions were enough.

Soon, a rumpled Sam was hauled into the kitchen by a chipper Ellory. Their hair was a straw pile of crisscrossed strands. Deep purple circles rimmed their eyes.

"How'd you sleep, Sam?" I asked as casually as I could.

Sam looked at me, their eyes glittering in bright accusation. "I was awake most of the night," they said.

Ellory gasped, "Oh no! Was it not quiet enough here?"

Sam shook their head. "No, it was plenty quiet, except for the rain and that same noise I was following before the storm." They then held out a hand to me. When I opened my palm, they dropped the single dried pea into its folds. "Found this before the birds started singing." They shrugged. "Got a few hours of sleep then."

Ellory looked at my hand, trying to see what had been passed between us. I closed my fist and suppressed a grin. "We didn't sweep the floor carefully enough, it seems."

"I swept it myself! I swept it extra!" Ellory was aghast. She was embarrassed that I'd suggest her cleaning skills weren't enough for Sam.

Sam ruefully smiled and shook their head. "No, you swept great. This was a test." They looked at me, their eyes darting across my face, flickering with eye contact for just an instant. "Did I pass?"

I looked at Rufus, who was standing there, drinking his tea, and listening to the whole exchange. He grinned a little from inside that deep beard.

"I'd say you did, Sam. I'm Rufus." He held out a giant calloused hand to the slim Sensitive.

Sam shook the offered hand awkwardly, their eyes focused on the teacup. "You have coffee?"

"It's homemade tea," I said. "I'll get you a cup, see if you can stand it."

15

WHENCE COMES OSRIC?

Have you ever stared at your own reflection so long it ceased to make sense? Where your eyes and mouth drift in some vague form that should be a face, but no longer is? Where you are so disconnected from that visage that it is no longer human, let alone your own? I imagine that is the strange floating sensation that Narcissus felt at the water's edge. Now, sitting among the reeds, my skirts already growing wet and heavy, my face assembles and reassembles itself in the rippling surface of the water. It has become a nonsense of a face. It is the last time I'll see it like this, wreathed in dark curls and scarlet ribbons. Echoes of the last few months ring in my mind, louder than the birdsong overhead.

It all started when the prince came to my room, with a face as white as milk. A haunted look behind his eyes, and dark circles below them. Gazing, now, at my own reflection, I see the same traces of horror. The same anguish of filial duty. He could not tell me – or anyone – that he had seen a spectre. But I rest convinced that he did. Just like I did.

It is the only thing that makes sense of his ramblings, of his rage, of his terror. Of my own apparent madness.

.   .   .

"Ophelia," my beloved father had said just a few weeks ago, "walk you here." He had thrust a book into my hands. "Read on this book that show of such an exercise may color your loneliness..." He rambled on a bit, muttering with the King and Queen, as the three of them hid behind the tapestries just beyond where I was instructed to read. After my mother's death, my best way of dealing with my father was obedience. Though I had always been relatively headstrong, it only created strife in our small, heartbroken household. Without Laertes at home to stick up for me against him, I had no choice but do whatever he told me to do. I regret not speaking with him more.

The book in my hands had not been a devotional. It was a copy of stories from the Orient, and I opened it at random to a page where another vizier's daughter was volunteering to be wed to the King, though it would forfeit her own life. She had a sister to support her. Laertes had been far away in France and not here to cleverly ask me to tell stories and delay my demise. A pang of loss chimed in my heart. I missed my brother. Though a greater loss hovered near.

I had heard the prince's gait before he entered the hall. I had been the bait in a trap set to snare him, of course he was headed that direction. My heart raced as I pretended to read about Scheherazade telling a tale of adventure and a stolen ring and a lamp that contained a djinn.

"To be, or not to be, that is the question," the prince seemed to be talking to himself. He was still so handsome, even though deep purple shadows hovered beneath his eyes. He paced distractedly as he spoke. "Whether 'tis nobler in the mind to suffer the slings and arrows of outrageous fortune, or to take arms against a sea of troubles and by opposing end them. To die, to sleep – no more – and by a sleep to say we end the heartache and the thousand natural shocks that flesh is heir to." Prince Hamlet's gaze finally seemed to focus on the room he was in. My heart leapt against my ribcage when he saw me sitting there.

"To die," he clarified, seemingly for my benefit, "to sleep, perchance to dream. Ay, there's the rub, for in that sleep of death what dreams may come, when we have shuffled off this mortal coil, must give us pause." His face looked haunted. His eyes held wordless horror. These words that made no sense to me at the moment have echoed in my mind for weeks. What dreams, indeed, do the dead suffer?

Hamlet approached me. I had once thought he loved me. He had looked on me with an admiring gaze. He had seemed to value my opinions, once. "There's the respect that makes calamity of so long life. For who would bear the whips and scorns of time, th' oppresor's wrong, the proud man's contumely, the pangs," he took my hand, "of disprized love...." His hand was cold and dry, like a corpse.

Dropping my hand, Hamlet sighed and looked off to the throne room, where he assumed his uncle, the King, might be. "The law's delay, the insolence of office, and the spurns of patient merit of th' unworthy takes, when he himself his quietus make with a bare bodkin?" His hand touched the hilt of the dagger in his belt as he gazed into the middle distance, seemingly forgetting me again. It had hurt my feelings, to be forgotten so easily. It felt like that was often the case, and not just with the prince. "Who would fardels bear, to grunt and sweat under a weary life, but that the dread of something after death. The undiscovered country from whose bourne no traveler returns, puzzles the will, and makes us rather bear those ills we have than fly to others that we know not of?"

The pale, haunted horror had returned to his visage, and I nearly gasped with it. With the wisdom borne of experience and memory, I could guess at exactly the mystery had the prince glimpsed that he thought so keenly of death and what rests beyond it, but in that moment, I could not understand any part of it. "Thus conscience does make cowards of is all; and thus the native hue of resolution is sicklied o'er with the pale cast of thought, and enterprises of great pitch and moment with this regard their currents turn awry and lose the name of action." He heaved a sigh, and his gaze returned again to the room, again to settle upon me. The book forgotten in my lap, I watched him. "Soft you now, the fair Ophelia. Nymph, in thy orisons be all my sins remembered."

· · ·

I WOULD CONTINUE to pray for him, my strange prince, and he knew it. Until he killed my father. "Good my lord," I ventured, "How does your honor for this many a day?" My father had kept me from responding to his letters, from speaking to the prince. I had missed him, then. At that time, I was certain the King and Queen were correct, that he was indeed mad. Speaking of death, of killing himself! Speaking of potential horror in the afterlife instead of the promise of salvation. In the moment, I willed myself not to tremble in fear of his distress.

Now, my face a distant memory in the water's edge, now, I know that Hamlet was no more mad than I am. He had simply glimpsed beyond the veil and was likely forced to do a bidding from beyond.

"I HUMBLY THANK YOU; WELL," he lied, "well," he tried again, "well." He shrugged as if the word were meaningless.

"My lord," I remembered what my father had instructed me to do. Reluctantly obedient, I could not forget the people hidden behind the tapestry, listening to every word we said. "I have remembrances of yours, that I have longed to redeliver. I pray you, now receive them." I handed him the ribbons and small necklace he had gifted me with his letters just a few weeks prior.

"No, not I. I never gave you aught." He closed his eyes. I watched the horror chase across his features once more. When he opened his eyes again, they were full of fear and worry. My own dread grew, reflected by his. I had been so stung by those words. I suspect he was trying to protect me.

"My honored lord, you know right well you did, and with them words of so sweet breath composed as made the things more rich. Their perfume lost, take these again, for to the noble mind rich gifts wax poor when givers prove unkind. There, my lord." I thrust them into his hands. He looked both heartbroken and angry at once.

"Ha ha!" his laugh was cruel. "Are you honest?"

"My lord?"

"Are you fair?"

"What means your lordship?"

"That if you be honest and fair, your honesty should admit no discourse to your beauty."

"Could beauty, my lord, have better commerce than with honesty?"

"Ay, truly, for the power of beauty will sooner transform honesty from what it is to a bawd than the force of honesty can translate beauty into his likeness. This was sometime a paradox, but now the time gives it proof. I did love you once." His face was briefly tender with the admission before the expression grew angry again.

"Indeed, my lord, you made me believe so." I had hesitated to admit it, but I remembered the ears behind the tapestry.

"You should not have believed me, for virtue cannot so inoculate our old stock but we shall relish of it. I loved you not." He was being cruel now. No more tenderness was available in his eyes.

"I was the more deceived." I did not try to swallow the rising tears. He expected them. As did our listeners.

"Get thee to a nunnery." He spat the words in disgust. "Why wouldst thou be a breeder of sinners?" He pulled me to my feet and gazed into my eyes from beneath a furrowed brow. "I am myself indifferent honest, but yet I could accuse me of such things that it were better my mother had not borne me: I am very proud, revengeful, ambitious, with more offenses at my beck than I have thoughts to put them in, imagination to give them shape, or time to act them in. What should such fellows as I do crawling between earth and heaven?" Still scowling, he brushed the side of my face with the backs of his fingers. "We are arrant knaves all; believe none of us. Go thy ways to a nunnery," he said. The tears were springing to my eyes fully, but I could feel his intent. He wanted to protect me from the things he'd seen, and from whatever it was he had become or was about to do. Before I could reply, he asked, "Where's your father?"

"At home, my lord," I lied, and Hamlet knew me well enough to know I was lying.

"Let the doors be shut upon him, that he may play the fool nowhere but in 's own house. Farewell." He stalked toward the door, turning his back upon me.

"O, help him, you sweet heavens!" the small prayer had burst from my lips. I had loved him once, and he had once loved me. Now, we are both the pawns of dead men.

"If thou dost marry;" the prince said, spinning on his heel with a new thought. "I'll give thee this plague for thy dowry; be thou as chaste as ice, as pure as snow, thou shalt not escape calumny." His voice grew louder and more tremulous with fury. "Get thee to a nunnery, farewell. Or if thou wilt needs marry, marry a fool, for wise men know well enough what monsters you make of them. To a nunnery, go, and quickly too. Farewell."

Softer, almost to myself, I said, "Heavenly powers, restore him!" the tears streaked down my cheeks, I did not remember that my cosmetics may be streaking. I do not know why he was so adamant that I never marry, or that I marry someone foolish. I would never make a monster of a man, but he'd seemed to blame me –

"I have heard of your paintings, too, well enough. God that given you one face, and you make yourselves another." The prince took his thumb and scraped it through the line of my tears to smudge the pink blush underneath it. "You jig, you amble, and you lisp, you nickname God's creatures, and make your wantonness your ignorance. Go to, I'll no more on't; it hath made me mad. I say we will have no more marriage. Those that are married already -- all but one – shall live. The rest shall keep as they are. To a nunnery, go."

There, on that cloudy day, I could not fathom which marriage the prince so deeply wished to disrupt. "O, what a noble mind is here o'erthrown!" I moaned a little to myself. He was not insane, though. He was upset. He had seen something – something he dared not tell me about, but that caused him endless horror. He had learned something about the betrayal of a woman – it wasn't me – but it was close enough to me that he had spurned me, me and marriage in general. "And I, of ladies most deject and wretched, that sucked the honey of his music vows, now see that noble and most sovereign reason like sweet bells jangled out of tune and harsh..."

The book rested open on the bench beside me, and I saw a segment of the page where the caliph decided to spare Scheherazade's life just one night, so he might learn the rest of the story. "O, woe is me, t' have seen what I have seen, see what I see!" I wept then in earnest, even though I could hear the rustle of tapestry and the approach of my father.

I'd ignored the king's conversation with my father about what they had overheard. They agreed he was not madly in love with me but were not sure if he was mad at all. Only vexed and troubled by something large. I kept the book. Perhaps Scheherazade's cleverness could aid *this* vizier's daughter, her Danish sister many times removed.

My own clever ruse begun, I slide a little further into the water, braiding flowers. Making sure Horatio is still lurking among the trees, I begin to sing.

It had been a while since Hamlet had yelled at me to closet myself away from him and the world of men. Father had bid me stay home, to prevent the prince from suffering more with my presence. But there were players in the castle, and there were to be merry entertainments. Finally, father had relented and let me visit, to see the play.

I had taken my customary seat, set away from the main throne room. I don't enjoy drawing attention to myself, since the prince was inconsistent with what form that attention might take.

"Come hither, my dear Hamlet, sit by me," the Queen said. Queen Gertrude had looked lovely in the flickering light of the evening. She had a few gems shining at her wrists and throat. I remember holding back a sigh.

"No, good Mother, here's metal more attractive." The prince turned instead to me and rested on the floor beside my feet. I did not take the pleasure in this that I would have a few weeks prior. "Lady, shall I lie in your lap?" he asked me.

"No, my lord." It was unseemly and annoying. Why would he think he could be so familiar with me after being so cruel?

"I mean, my head upon your lap?" He asked again, trying to seem innocent. For a moment, it was as if the old Hamlet had returned. The one who told me how beautiful I was, and how he burned for me.

I relented. "Ay, my lord."

He grinned wickedly then, "Do you think I meant country matters?" How rude! I had been thinking about his shouting at me to become a nun!

"I think nothing, my lord." I said, hesitant to wade into any such conversation with the prince.

"That's a fair thought to lie between a maid's legs." His voice was wry and droll.

Pretending not to get the joke, I asked, "What is, my lord?"

"Nothing." He emphasized the pun, and I rolled my eyes. But still, I was mystified by this change in his demeanor.

"You are merry, my lord." I tried not to make it a question. It was a question.

"Who, I?"

"Ay, my lord."

"O God, your only jig maker. What should a man do but be merry? For look you how cheerfully my mother looks, and my father died within's two hours." *Two hours*? How odd. Had he lost so many weeks? I know now how likely that was.

"Nay, 'tis twice two months, my lord."

"So long? Nay then, let the devil wear black, for I'll have a suit of sables. O heavens! Die two months ago, and not forgotten yet? Then there's hope a great man's memory may outlive his life half a year..." He prattled on for a moment, like my father used to tend to do. I got distracted by the players entering the stage.

Though Hamlet was talking with me, and cordially enough, I realized why he had chosen to sit with me. It was not my company he sought, but rather my location in the room. From my lap, he could watch the players and the King and Queen with barely a turn of his head. This seemed to be his larger purpose. I felt used, not attended. I was advantageous, not wanted.

As the players enacted their show with each perplexing theme following each confusing turn, Hamlet had nearly ceased watching the players at all. It was as if he knew what show they were performing and was watching for reactions among the audience. He still playfully flirted, but his heart wasn't in it. I could tell by where his gaze was drawn that he was thinking about his mother, and her quick marriage to his uncle.

I was lumped in with her as a fickle woman, or I was innocent and should become a nun to retain that innocence. He no longer saw me as myself, as a person in my own right. Even as his head warmed my knee, my heart broke a little more.

Now, now I let myself float and drift in the cool water. My now heavy skirts trap some air, to keep me above the surface. I play with a flower with one hand, singing nonsense. Horatio, still hidden in the shadows, cannot see my other hand, releasing the already-loose stays beneath me.

I had woken with a fright at the sound of moaning. Sitting up, I saw my father standing at the threshold to my bedroom door. My father, but *not* my father. A spectre of Polonius, not the man himself. I could see the wall beyond him through his mighty chest. I could see a pale light crowning him. I gasped in fear and tried to cover my eyes, but then the spectre spoke.

"My child. Ophelia."

"F-Father?" I trembled under my bedclothes. I wished that a maid or servant would dash in and startle away this vision.

"Remember the baker's daughter, Ophelia, though she has all that she desires she is stingy and will not share it with a poor man. She cannot see that in all poor men are the savior, and in the savior, there is blessing in charity. Do not be stingy with your loaf, Ophelia. Give it all unto the lord."

I knew the parable he was telling me, but it made no sense. Why would a ghost speak these words?

Why was my father in the form of a ghost and not his whole self, hale and alive in the next room?

"Do not become the owl, seeking the night for wisdom you once lacked."

"Father, wherefore art thou a spectre?"

"Slain!" He cried. "Slain by your once-beloved prince. Slain through a curtain in his mother's room."

He had hidden behind a curtain when he set me as bait for Hamlet. It was my father's favorite trick to learn things he could not otherwise discover. But in the Queen's rooms? The scandal was nearly enough to rock me from the fact that my father had been killed. Killed by Hamlet.

"Avenge me, daughter." My father continued.

"Call upon your brother, that he may too avenge me. Spurn the prince and pity the Queen, child. Give the lord of salvation all of the bread of your mercy." The spectre of my father had disappeared into the dim room, the pale light around him dissolved.

I did not sleep again that night. I haven't slept much since that night.

When I had gained control of my breath, and my heartbeat calmed to a more natural rhythm, I rose from my bed, and sat at the desk. My shaking hands lit the taper, and I penned a letter to Laertes in France. I would send it in the morning, after I'd confirmed my father's fate.

I could not bring myself to sorrow, but my mind darted like a rabbit from thought to thought.

"To sleep, perchance to dream" were the words that the prince had spoken. I paced my bedchamber. I thought again of the prince, entering my room in disarray, pale and sleepless. He had seen a ghost. Like me, it was likely the ghost of his father. Perhaps, like me, he had been commanded to wreak some vengeance.

But he, he who I had sought to understand, was the one my father's ghost demanded vengeance against. Why not the Queen? Had she known he was secreted behind the curtain? Had she no power to stop his killing?

I held the warring emotions of grief and outrage in my heart. Terror and vengeance. Sleepless, pacing, and full of emotions I could share with no one, I pulled at my hair. The prince, the prince would be able to talk with me about what I had seen. But the prince was whom I was supposed to kill – to avenge my father.

Was there no solace? No peace?

Pacing in my room that night, I realized that Ophelia was powerless to do what her father had asked. Yes, she could write to her brother. But she was not in a position to avenge her father. Not a mere girl.

I had known, known in my bones, that Horatio would not try to save me. Laertes had said that my whole plan was destroyed if so. I drift with the current and sing a little more loudly. Horatio does not move from his place in the trees.

While I waited for Laertes, I planted seeds of my vengeance. I planted seeds of my madness, which, like the prince, was not madness at all. I planted thoughts in the ears of those who heard me, whether they knew it or not. I watered the seeds with reckless tears. And I avoided the Prince and Queen until I received notice that my brother was drawing near to home.

A gentleman I did not recognize granted me audience with the Queen. She was speaking still with Horatio. Horatio was a friend of Hamlet, not a friend of mine. It is impossible to sup at the same table as often as we had and not make acquaintance. But we shared no words or kind thoughts with one another.

I feigned my madness and distraction as I approached. "Where is the beauteous majesty of Denmark?"

"How now, Ophelia?"

I'd allowed my hair to grow matted and tangled. I used no cosmetics to mask how little I'd been sleeping. And deliberately, in audience with the Queen, I sang like a child.

"How should I your true love know
From another one

By his cockle hat and staff,

And his sandal shoon."

"Alas, sweet lady, what imports this song?" The Queen was aghast.

"Say you? Nay, pray you, mark. He is dead and gone, lady, he is dead and gone; at his head a grass-green turf, at his heels a stone. Oho!" She had been there when my father was slain. She must have known that he was hiding behind curtains in her chamber. Hamlet blamed the Queen for her role in his father's death. I blamed Gertrude for the same.

I rambled on for a while, intermittently singing and speaking nonsense. The King came and pretended to be baffled at my grief. I pretended to be addle-pated and wrecked by my emotions – I had lost the love the Prince. I had lost the love of my Father.

"How do you, pretty lady?" The king asked me, and I wanted to scream. I wanted to shout. Instead, I remembered the parable the ghost of my father had spoken to me.

"Well, God 'ild you! They say the owl was a baker's daughter. Lord, we know what we are, but know not what we may be. God be at your table!" Perhaps the King was as much to blame for my state as the Queen was.

"Pray let's have no words of this; but when they ask you what it means, say you this: "Tomorrow is Saint Valentine's day, all in the morning betime, and I a maid at your window, to be your Valentine. Then up he rose, and donned his clothes, and dupped the chamber door. Let in the maid, that out a maid Never departed more." I know that they thought I was speaking of Hamlet. Perhaps, they might misconstrue some debauchery on his part. However, however, I was telling them the trick. I could not avenge my father as myself. I could not avenge my father as a maid. I would have to become something else.

I planted seeds of worry in their minds, whether they realized it or not. I planted seeds of worry, and I planted seeds of my plan. "I hope all will be well." I told them. "We must be patient, but I cannot choose but to week to think they would lay him i' the cold ground.

My brother shall know if it. And so I thank you for your good counsel. Come, my coach! Good night, ladies, good night, sweet ladies, good night, good night." With more rambling songs and a lost look, I wandered out of the room. But not far enough to miss the King telling Horatio to watch me.

Horatio's eyes have haunted me as much as my father's ghost since that day. Watching. Lurking. Like an ever-present stink of death. I grew to hate him in those few days.

My brother knew my plan before his arrival. He knew of our father's death and of the ghost's demand to avenge him. Like Scheherazade's sister must aid her in her plan, my brother had to be part of my own plans of vengeance.

He may have laid it on a little thick in front of the King, though.

"O heat, dry up my brains! Tears seven times salt burn out the sense and virtue of mine eye! By heaven, thy madness shall be paid with weight till our scale turn to beam. O rose of May!" He was pouring on his anguish a little melodramatically for my taste, but I hid my smirk by braiding a flower into my ratted hair. "Dear maid, kind sister, sweet Ophelia! O heavens, is't possible a young maid's wits should be as mortal as an old man's life? Nature is fine in love, and where 'tis fine it sends some precious instance of itself after the thing it loves."

I wanted the King to make no mistake that I was driven mad by my father's death. I sang, "They bore him barefaced on the bier, Hey nonny, nonny, hey nonny, and in his grave rained many a tear –" then abruptly broke off the song "Fare you well, my dove." If only the ghost of that dove had let me sleep.

"Hadst thou thy wits and didst persuade revenge, it could not move thus." Laertes might have trod a little close to the truth with that one.

"You must sing "a-down a-down," and you "call him a-down-a." O, how the wheel becomes it! It is the false steward that stole his master's daughter."

"This nothing's more than matter." And thus we played back and forth, my portrayal of madness deepening, his portrayal of woe growing. The tale had be told to the King and Queen to make the plan work. Together, my brother and I watered the seeds that I'd already planted.

"Do you see this, O God?" my brother wailed as I left the chamber.

"Laertes, I must commune with your grief..." I heard the King begin to speak, and I meandered away from the palace, pretending to be addled.

The dark-haired village girl who died of pox last night will be buried in greater state than she had ever hoped.

I make sure Horatio watches me sink below the water as I sing. I make sure he witnesses Ophelia's sad suicide and I let my gowns drift and sink above me as I swim into the reeds. I take the reed I'd plucked earlier, and I use it like a straw, sipping air from the surface. Staying underwater until my lips turn blue and my skin grows cold.

I do not rise from the reeds until I'm sure that Horatio is gone and no longer watching for me. Shivering, I retrieve the bag of clothing from the bank. A young man's clothes.

I chop off my wet hair and leave it strewn in the water, wrenching the garlands of flowers free.

I draw my gown out of the brook and dress the village girl's corpse. I'd left her in the water, out of Horatio's sight, to allow her body to bloat a little. Now, when they fished Ophelia out of the brook, they wouldn't know the difference. I put the garlands of flowers carefully in her dark hair.

Her face and my face swim again into nonsense. Ophelia is dead, she is in my arms.

The guards from the palace come running down to the shore. Sent by Horatio, too late to help poor Ophelia. They help me drag the girl's body to the higher ground.

"Who are you?" one of the guards asks.

"Osric," I tell him. "A friend of Laertes."

16

A YEAR

Boss brought Dunya to one of the parties. We didn't have a chance to talk, and I couldn't get her near any of the dark zones I'd created for the cameras. But we hugged. She got to see that I was still alive, and that she was an Auntie. She got to meet her nephew.

My husband didn't notice her. He didn't notice much. I was not certain he realized he had a son.

He left me alone to pray after his son was born, though. I'm not sure why. He didn't join me. I wasn't sure if he was an atheist or an infidel. He never made that clear. The wedding had been Muslim for my sake, I believed.

It was stressful. Having myself and a baby to keep alive. To nurse while I read him the next wild concocted tale from the program. Some of them seemed familiar, but twisted at odd angles as the machine learned how to morph and recombine the stories I had fed it. I spent some of my days reprogramming the system to draw in even more types of stories, to build even more combinations.

The baby slept best when I was telling stories of love. I adjusted the code to tell those a bit more often.

17

IF HORSES WERE GILDED, FALADA WOULD SHINE

Though the horseless carriage had begun to rattle and roar through streets, a good horse was still an important means of transportation in those days. Bicycles still carried the stain of impropriety for a young lady. Cleo was only ever a proper young lady. She remained true to her horse, Falada, even when her suitors arrived in their noisy, exciting automobiles.

Cleo had bobbed her hair and loved the swinging freedom of its weight around her chin, the relief of the heavy knot at the back of her head. Falada, on the other hand, had a long creamy sweep of mane and tail, combed to silky smoothness every day. Her palomino coat was brushed to the point of gleaming, even on the days Cleo did not ride her. Even her opal-colored hooves were shiny.

Though Falada noticed long lines of men in dark coats waiting for jobs, or bread, or something, the economic turmoil of the city did not enter her stable. Her family, her Cleo, seemed to be protected somehow from the sorrow and despair that scented the streets. She noticed, however, that they rode less in town. There were fewer trips to the park. They stayed on their own handful of acres, or they went all the way out to the countryside, instead.

Falada didn't notice the parties in the big house much. Only that there were fewer guests in her barn. The open stalls often stayed unused for months at a time. And they took the large one at the end of the stable to house a belching, smelly automobile.

These were the days before Falada could talk. She was simply a horse. A smart, caring horse, to be sure. But still, only a horse, whose main love was her golden-haired girl.

"We will be moving house in a few weeks," her golden girl told her as she brushed her mane one dusty afternoon. Falada's eyes were half closed. She rested her weight on her right back hoof, letting the left leg hang slack for a few minutes. "I'm engaged to be married, and you're coming with me, Falada." The news woke her up. It wasn't unusual for Cleo to tell Falada the goings on of her life. Sometimes she wept into Falada's mane. Sometimes she shared her thoughts, having no one else to share them with. The comb was gentle in her mane, tugging a little at a time.

"I won't get to meet him until we reach his country estate. Mother says my betrothed is the bees' knees." It was one of those afternoons where her Cleo would share everything that was on her mind. Falada flickered an ear in her direction so she knew she was listening. "I'm nervous about that part."

"Mother is hiring a maid for me, someone to help me prepare for the trip, and to be a companion for me when I get to the estate – it's very far out in the countryside, you know." Falada didn't know. But she was always up for an adventure, especially if her Cleo would be there. "There are so many people out of work, Mother says it is a kindness to employ a person."

The young woman stood close to Falada's jaw as she combed her forelock. "Mother also gave me a good luck charm," Cleo held a white handkerchief up so Falada could see it. There were three spots of blood, crimson against the white lace. "She said this is so her love will continue to protect me in my new life."

Falada's yellow quilted blanket was stifling and too warm in the springtime sun. She suffered the indignity of standing in a metal box and being drawn behind the roar of the automobile. She did not wish to suffer from the further indignity of her satiny palomino coat being dark and rusty with sweat and foam when she arrived at her new home. But there was little she could do about that in the metal box.

She shifted her weight to try to keep her sides from touching the walls of the box. Falada tried very hard not to sigh, because that meant breathing in the smelly fumes of the rattling vehicle that pulled her box. It was an unpleasant, uncanny smell. And an unpleasant, uncanny feeling to be moving without moving her own legs.

When her Cleo finally allowed her to back out of the box down a very unsafe-feeling ramp, Falada realized that this was not her new stable. It was not her new home. They were merely stopping and taking a break. Cleo and her dark-haired serving girl, Mildred, sat on a blanket beside a stream. Falada was relieved of her too-warm blanket, and allowed to wade into the stream for a drink.

"Please fetch me a cup of water," Cleo asked Mildred. Falada turned her left ear toward their conversation. Cleo was holding out a small golden cup for the girl to fill.

"If you are thirsty," said the serving girl, snatching the cup from Cleo's hand, "Then go to the stream yourself, and lie down and drink out of the water like your horse. I didn't choose to be your servant. I have to move far away from my family to work for you. To be stuck in the middle of the countryside where nothing ever happens! For what? A job." Mildred grasped a hunk of tasty green grass from the ground and shredded it with her fingers.

Falada saddened to see her Cleo following the cruel girl's instructions. She flickered her sensitive ears when a tiny voice in the young woman's pocket whispered, "If this your mother knew, her heart would break in two."

They continued along the journey to her Cleo's new home until they stopped by another stream, and the conversation repeated itself. Cleo asked for a drink, and the girl, who used the golden cup herself, refused to help her. Cleo, again, leaned down over the stream. And Falada, from where she stood, drinking nearby, heard the tiny voice whispering, "If this your mother knew, her heart would break in two."

However, the little handkerchief, which Falada was certain had spoken those words, slipped out of Cleo's blouse as she bent to the stream! Falada hurried to the little white cloth with its three red dots, and she ate it right up, swallowing it whole before it rushed away in the stream. Her Cleo saw her do this, and stroked her shoulder, telling her what a good girl she was. How Falada would be both friend and good luck to her now, on her journey.

Before they got back into the automobile, Mildred crossed her arms and stood, staring at Cleo with a frown. "I don't want to move to the countryside. But if I were rich like you, then your betrothed would take me on automobile drives to the city. I could go to parties!" Falada watched with the confusion and understanding only a horse can provide, as the serving-girl forced Cleo to exchange her fringed, knee-length dress for Mildred's long, drab one. The angry girl seemed to rain threats down upon her Cleo, raising her fists, and shouting. The humans traded every garment, down to Cleo's shiny shoes and her beautiful pearl necklace. Falada watched as Cleo swore to tell no one at their destination about this change in circumstances. She swore on her own life, and on Falada's life, that she would speak to no living soul about this arrangement. It was alarming, but Falada was only a horse. The handkerchief within her first stomach wept bitterly for Cleo's broken-hearted mother.

In the trailer, rattling along behind the noisy automobile, Falada realized that the handkerchief was magical indeed. As she shifted her weight from hoof to hoof on the bumpy road, Falada began to speak. At first, she was simply muttering to herself, complaining about the trailer as a means of travel, about the bumpiness of the road, about the smelliness of the automobile. Then, she realized that she could talk just like her Cleo. She would be able to communicate with her! She could even tell someone at their destination the tale of the betrayal of the serving girl.

~

THE STALL FALADA had been given was spacious and piled with sweet-smelling straw and sawdust. The stable was beautiful and warm, with at least a dozen other horses. Falada had never seen such a palatial stable, its loft full of hay and roly-poly kittens. The smelly, noisy auto-mobiles were stabled in another building away from the horses. Even the offensive metal box was hauled somewhere else on the vast estate.

Her Cleo wore the garb of the plain serving girl. Falada watched out her stall door as the golden-haired girl fed the birds in the stable yard, instead of living inside the grand white building over the hill. Her Cleo was spreading grain from her apron, bitterly sad. The one joy in her new life was that when her chores were done, she could visit Falada in her stall, and brush and comb her like always.

"Cleo, you are brought low," Falada broke her silence, speaking with the magic of the handkerchief. "If this your mother knew, her heart would break in two."

Cleo stopped brushing Falada's shoulder. "Falada, did you just... speak?"

Falada bobbed her head, and then tried again, "Cleo, I did."

The brush resumed, softly against Falada's shoulder. She waited.

"You saw what happened, back at the stream."

"I did, but who would take the testimony of a horse?" Falada asked.

Cleo grunted as she moved the brush further down Falada's body. They lapsed into silence together, enjoying the softness of touch and the whispers of the brushes.

An enormous clatter rose at the stable door. Suddenly, in rushed Mildred, wearing Cleo's favorite riding clothes. Behind her were servants and a handsome young man, also dressed for riding.

"Saddle my horse, girl," Mildred told Falada's Cleo. Cleo lowered her gaze and set about the barn, preparing to saddle Falada for the wretched maid.

Falada would have none of that.

She did not speak – only with her Cleo – but as soon as the vile girl mounted her, Falada began to twitch and buck. She reared and shimmied and danced. She tried jerky, unexpected movements. Old Mildred was not an accomplished rider. Not like Cleo. Falada unseated her once, twice. On the third time, Falada managed to land the maid's rump in a wide puddle of mud with a satisfying splat.

Furious, Mildred commanded that Falada be killed. Slain. And to prove that they hadn't merely sold Falada to a neighbor, she demanded in a shrill voice that Falada's head be hung over the arched gate that led from the great house out to the yard where the poultry was fed every day, beside the great stone well. Falada knew this was cruelty against her Cleo. But there was little she could do to protect her.

Death. Death was not surprising to Falada. She was a horse, not a human.

What was surprising, however, was that the handkerchief still worked its magic within her. She could still see out of her glassy eyes, and she could still speak.

Early one morning, her lovely Cleo gazed up at her head on the arch, her apron still full of feed, and the poultry nagging and scolding around her ankles.

"Alas, Falada, hanging there," she said up to her horse.

Falada looked down at her Cleo, and if she had a body to weep with, she would have wept. She replied, "Alas, my Cleo, how ill you fare." And the handkerchief within Falada completed the rhyme unbidden, "if this your mother knew, her heart would break in two."

Each day, Falada watched people come and go through her archway. She watched the evil Mildred try to ride more docile horses. She watched the young man – who was supposed to marry her Cleo – screw his face up in determination to do what was asked of him. He never spoke to the lowly maiden with golden hair who fed the poultry.

Once, Falada overheard a conversation between the young man and his father, striding through the barn yard to saddle up for a hunt.

"She is not who you said she would be," the young man told his father.

The older man nodded. "She is not who I thought she would be."

"I cannot go through with it."

The old man sighed, and though they strode out of Falada's earshot, she could tell the older man was trying to reassure the younger. She gave it no more thought, however, because her Cleo was passing through her arch.

"Falada, Falada, you are dead, and all the joy in my life has fled," her Cleo said.

Falada looked down at the sad, beloved face. "Alas, alas if your mother knew, her loving heart would break in two," she replied. Immediately, she regretted speaking, as the old man was standing in the shadow of the barn door, and he'd heard Falada speak. She feared there would be consequences for that.

Later in the day, the old man wandered back toward the barn alone. He lingered near the well until Falada's Cleo arrived to fetch water for the animals in the stable.

"Dear girl," the old man said, his voice gentle. "What woes do you have that you might share? You look so sad."

Cleo bowed her head and averted her gaze. She looked at the bucket in her hand. "Sir, I have sworn on my life to never speak of them to another living soul. I cannot tell you."

Falada wished that the king would turn some trick. Maybe he could get the girl to confess her tale to an inanimate object, so no living soul would hear it. She could tell the tale to a stovepipe or to a well, but alas. That was not to be. He was very old. And the next day the staff had arm bands of black cloth, and the house began arranging for his funeral.

The young man strode in and out of the barn several times that day, frustrated with the responsibilities heaped upon him. Weighed down by the grief of his father's death.

Falada knew that her Cleo could help him. That the disarray of the house was because of Mildred. She knew this in her long-buried heart. Finally, when the young man walked through her arch alone, and when no one else was in the stable yard, Falada chanced to speak.

"Young man, young man, whose world has gone foul, you must find the truth of lies to right betrayal." Her rhyme wasn't perfect, but it was enough to make him spin on his heel and gaze up at her. He looked at Falada as if he was seeing her for the first time.

"How can I learn the truth, dear horse?" He asked up to Falada's head on the arch, "What would right this ship's course?" He tried, thinking perhaps the rhyme was important.

Falada guided him to a smooth grey-green rock that rested on the ground beside the well. She taught him that the old man had conspired to make this stone speak the truth. That it could tell him everything. Falada suggested that he rest the rock beside his bed, and have his bride use it as a stepping stool.

The young man took her advice, heaving the rock into his arms, and carrying it into the big house behind Falada's arch.

The next person in the courtyard was the vile serving-maid, Mildred, still dressed in Cleo's finery. Falada waited until she, too, was alone in the yard. Then she spoke.

"Wicked girl, the truth is near," she warned her. "Your betrothed has magic that will tell him whether the woman entering his bed is a maiden or not." The girl's eyes grew as big as horseshoes, and she scuttled out of the barnyard. Falada wasn't sure what Mildred's plans were, but she discovered it soon enough.

Mildred cornered Cleo in the barnyard, and Falada watched as her plan unfolded. The serving-maid demanded that Cleo climb into the betrothed's bed at night, and then Mildred would switch with her before he woke each morning. This was how the maid thought to circumvent the magic knowledge the young man might possess.

Cleo agreed to this strange arrangement, bowing her head.

For three mornings, her Cleo came back to the stable yard to feed the poultry having spent half the night in the young man's bed, untouched. Falada watched the birds around her Cleo's ankles. Other people stirred, so they could not discuss the strange events of the evening.

On the third day, the young man strode into the barnyard, his face full of thunder, his brows drawn low. Mildred followed after him, pleading, "It's not what you think!"

The man stopped before Cleo, just under Falada's chin. "You are the maiden who is in my bed each night," he said to Cleo. Falada saw her head jerk back in surprise. Mildred tried to wedge herself between the two.

"She's not! It's me! You know you wake up beside me!"

The young man glanced up at Falada and shook his head. "No, the stone beside my bed told me everything," he told her. "You are not a maiden, but she is."

Falada would have smiled if horses could smile.

"And," the young man looked from one girl's face to the other, "You're the servant, and she is my betrothed!" His voice was triumphant.

Falada laughed.

Mildred blanched white in horror. Falada knew her laughter overhead just made the girl more nervous.

"She's a lowly maid!" Mildred said, her pointing finger like a claw. "If a lowly maid were to pretend to be a rich woman, it would be a horrible crime! Worth flogging! Worth death!"

The young man turned, his eyebrows raised at the serving-maid. "Indeed," he said. "If she were masquerading as someone she was not, how should I punish her, exactly?"

"She should be put in a barrel spiked with nails and dragged behind horses until she is dead." Mildred pronounced, ready to heap a final indignity and pain upon Falada's poor Cleo.

But the young man was savvy. He knew the maid's treachery. He looked up at Falada.

"What say you, has she pronounced her own sentence?"

"As surely as my true mistress speaks not a word," Falada replied to him.

These were modern times, with short dresses, short hair, and roaring automobiles. But there were still barrels and nails. And there were still horses that could drag that barrel.

The next time Falada saw Cleo, she was dressed in her own proper clothing, her golden hair gleaming in the sun. She walked with the young man, and they were well-matched in temperament and beauty.

Falada herself could not die. She could not even spit out the magical handkerchief. But she became known as a font of wisdom. And people from far and wide would travel to her and share their woes with the talking horse above the gate to the stable yard.

18

ELLA'S EQUILIBRIUM

No one ever asked Ella whether she liked doing her chores back at home. The palace was lovely. She quite enjoyed being far away from her stepmother and her stepsisters. But Ella missed her routine. She missed the grounding of doing something with her hands and body. She missed the satisfaction of sitting back, sweaty and tired, and seeing a job well done gleaming before her. She missed being Cinderella.

As the whirl of the palace life surrounded the Princess Ella, she found herself lost in thoughts and daydreams far more often than she had in her woeful days at her stepmother's heel. Her head floated above her – distant from her body. The strange clothing expected of a princess felt alien on her skin.

She could not get to the linden tree her mother planted in the garden back at her stepmother's home. She had no idea how to summon or locate her fairy godmother from within the palace. Ella was alone, bereft, and disconnected from herself in her new, strange life.

She walked in the manicured gardens without watching her step – the paths were so carefully trimmed into straight lines. Instead of looking at the flowers around her, she gazed at the sky, trying to tell what shapes the clouds had become. While she was lost in this reverie, a bluebird found her, and rested upon her shoulder.

"Oh! Shoo!" Ella's serving maid Annie cried, waving her hands at the bird.

"Leave it be," Ella stopped Annie's commotion. She looked at the bird. "Perhaps he's here to help me." But the bird had no seeds to sort from the ashes. It had no messages from her fairy godmother. She was on her own, it seemed. Or she could simply no longer understand what it was trying to tell her.

Ella drifted through the days, waiting for her gown to be ready for the royal wedding. They surrounded her with maids and courtiers, people eager to serve her or to be her companions. None of them acted as if they knew who she had been, or the life she had been used to, before.

One afternoon, just after she had tried on dozens of shoes for the wedding – none of them fit her properly – she concentrated on the effort of reading a book when a mouse wearing a tiny tunic skittered across her stockinged foot.

She jumped, startled. But did not kick. She hoped no one saw her little friend. She could hear it squeaking under her skirt. She lifted the hem a little, and whispered, "What did you say?"

The mouse squeaked frantically, squeaked at length. But instead of words, Ella heard squeaking sounds. Without the miniature yellow tunic, she would have never identified the mouse as one of her friends from her former life. Frustrated, the mouse stopped squeaking and ran away. She couldn't understand him at all.

Ella wept and wept that evening. The prince came to her and begged for her to be merry. He offered balls, shoes, and silver gowns. But she had those things. She didn't need them. She wanted to sweat. To feel her body move. To remember how powerful her arms were. She wanted to feel alive again, not drifting endlessly like a feather on a stream.

After her wedding, the prince and Ella shared rooms. But it did not help her feelings of disconnection. After months of feeling separated from herself, Ella made up her mind. She had to do something differently.

The prince was still snoring when she touched her small foot to the plush carpet beside their royal bed hours before they were expected to rise. Her steps fell without even a creak from the floor or a groan from the mattress. She wasn't sure whether she'd heard something, a faint rustling, perhaps, that had woken her. But Ella knew what she had to do. She padded to her dressing room as quietly as she could.

Silently, silently, she opened the small wooden trunk under the window. The small trunk held the items from her life before. A sewing kit, a few scraps of cloth, a brooch that belonged to her mother. Leaving the small, noisy, clattering items in the box, she lifted out her oldest, most tattered dress and apron. She combed her hair and tied it up in a scarf. Would anyone in the palace be fooled by this disguise? Surely not the prince himself, as this was how he found her the day he tried her shoe on every girl in the city. But not everyone here had seen her in her old life. The rustling sound happened again. Ella wondered if it was one of her mouse friends, but the dressing room floors were spotless, free of a tuft of dust.

Ella slipped back into the royal bedchamber and settled on her knees beside the cold hearth. She felt the cool of the marble seep into the skin of her knees and shins, the tops of her bare feet. She inhaled the familiar scent of the ashes, settled and soft and gray in the bottom of the fireplace. As quietly as she could, she removed the wrought iron tools from their rack beside the fireplace. Efficiently, she shoveled the cold ashes out of the fireplace and into their metal bucket. It was so satisfying, creating those little shovelfuls of papery, dusty ash. Dropping them into the bucket with a small gray puff. She used the stiff broom to sweep the remaining ash from the hearth, and she felt her heart rate drop as she worked. She felt her body grow heavy and dense.

She felt real for the first time in weeks. Breathing deeply, Ella closed her eyes. She sat back on her heels and let herself revel in the sensation.

The rustling sound grew louder. Glancing over her shoulder toward the noise, Ella gasped.

Her serving maid, Annie, gasped as well. Their eyes met. The women froze.

The petite brown-haired maid stood in her doorway, wearing the gown Ella had worn to a ball a few weeks prior. It was not as splendid as the gown her fairy godmother created, but that ethereal garment was gone after a distant midnight. This one was still splendid in its own way. It gleamed and sparkled with gemstones on shimmering satin. Hand-tatted lace overlaid the bodice with kissing lovebirds and flowers. The gown was much too long on Annie, it crumpled and folded around her ankles. The bodice had not been laced up, little Annie's curves spilled out of it at all angles.

For a few breathless moments, the only sound moving the air in the chamber the prince's snores.

While Annie may not be able to understand Ella's need to do a chore, to move her body, to be productive, Ella certainly understood Annie's desire. She remembered the longing to be dressed up and beautiful. To dance all evening at a ball. It was that desire that had called her fairy godmother.

With her connection to her godmother severed, Ella realized perhaps that godmotherly job had fallen to her.

She stood up from the hearth. When Annie started toward her, Ella pressed a finger to her lips and waved the girl back into her dressing room. They shut the dressing room door with a small click, leaving the snoring prince to sleep for a few more hours.

Behind the door, Ella smiled at Annie's mortified expression. The maid stammered and fluttered her hands, trying ineffectually to remove Ella's gown.

Ella steered Annie to her dressing table, where the mirror and hairbrush sat amid a few jewels and cosmetics. She pressed on the girl's shoulders without a word, urging her to sit down on the little padded stool. Annie's knees bent abruptly, seating her with a bounce.

Ella looked at Annie from where she stood behind her, meeting her gaze in the mirror. With a small smile, she leaned forward and grabbed the hairbrush. Annie flinched. Ella frowned.

"Oh, my lady, we must get you ready for your ball," the princess whispered to the maid.

Annie may have suffered at the hands of other members of the palace–Ella would be sternly investigating that later–but she wanted to brush the maid's hair. Unpinning her tidy braids, Ella ran the brush slowly and gently through Annie's hair, fussing over her. She straightened the gown on the girl's shoulders.

As she tutted over her, Annie relaxed bit by bit at the attention, the soft, soothing touches, the sweetness of being loved and pampered. The joy of seeing herself in a beautiful gown in the mirror. They both knew, without speaking, that this was temporary. That they would have to put on their other clothes and play those other roles as demanded by society. As Ella fit her sparkling tiara on Annie's dark hair, they smiled at each other. Both knowing, as well, that this was necessary.

19

VIVIEN'S HEIR

Handcuffing oneself to an ancient oak tree takes some creative problem-solving. I'm not bragging or anything. When I'd come up with this plan, I wasn't counting on having to do it alone. I'd expected other members of my family to be here to protect the tree. I rubbed my cheek against its bark, failing to dry my tears. The grinding of engines and motors reverberated up the hill, like they were going to saw through the ground itself – cut the hump of land off the face of the planet like a dodgy mole.

The tree had been huge, hollow, and old centuries ago. It had been like a tower since before time began, so now, now it was a monument of oakdom. It was impossible to think that the edifice had grown from a single acorn. Except for the garish pink spray-painted slash that marred the western face of its trunk, it was knobbly, massive, and perfect.

It was a sacred place to my family. At least, I thought it was. Perhaps it was only sacred to me. I'd been visiting this tree with my grandmother for as long as I could remember. -It was supposed to be safe. The estate was supposed to hold it in perpetuity. I listened to the chomping sounds of metal teeth eating the grove below me. I couldn't see the trees falling, but I could hear them.

The clattering treetops drowned out the sound of the small spring that trickled behind my right foot. I hoped the water gave me some form of magical strength. I didn't have a law degree. I didn't have any degree for that matter. Nothing I had ever learned or understood about the world could help protect this one sacred thing. But I had a body. Not a body I agreed with or felt particularly fond of. So I bought a long chain and two pairs of handcuffs and I came up here, determined to save the tree where my umpty-great-grandmother entombed the cursed body of my umpty-great-grandfather just after they had made love in its shelter. Our family line was descended from this union of enemies – of opposites – and it made us who we are.

Why the hell was I the only member of my family up there? I'd told my whole family. My family who hadn't spoken to me since I came out years ago. I'd told them all the time and date. I told them all my plan. We were supposed to create a living chain around the tree, all of us, united in our determination to protect this site of our heritage. The tree didn't care that I was crying against its surface, and it couldn't understand that my heart was breaking all over again. Over the sound of my family rejecting me, and our ancestor's grave along with me, I barely noticed the bulldozer pull over the crest of the hill.

"Hey! What are you doing?" A shout and a whistle sounded. The sounds of engines sputtered and purred to a halt. "What the fuck are you doing?"

I had a plan. It was a dumb plan. But it was still a plan. I swallowed my snot and I decided to stick to it, even though my family was supposed to help me. I had memorized the entire poem by Tennyson about Merlin and Vivien. My plan was to recite it in a show of theatrical solidarity with my tree. Like I said, it was a dumb plan.

A storm was coming, but the winds were still
And in the wild woods of Broceliande, before an oak
So hollow, huge and old it looked like a tower of ivied masonwork,
At Merlin's feet, the wily Vivien lay.

Tennyson's was my favorite version of the tale. Partially because there were family legends that we had shared the real story with him along the way. Of course, he got the location of the tree wrong. We were near the Cornish coast, not northern France.

"The fuck?"

"You can't have this tree. It's illegal to destroy a burial site, and this is where Merlin himself is buried."

"Merlin? The wizard?"

"Yes," I shifted and jingled my chains. "This is his gravesite, and you can't cut this tree down. You'll disturb his grave."

A man in an orange vest with a clipboard looked at me through the clear plastic lenses of his safety glasses. "Look, sir, um, er, miss," He grunted. "Look, you. You can't be here. And we're ordered to cut down every tree on this hill. For the houses."

"This is a grave site. Do you really want to have the ghost of Merlin haunting the people who live on this hill?" I asked the question seriously. I didn't doubt for a moment that my granddad-times-whatever could do that.

He blinked. Once. Slowly. I think maybe he was counting to ten.

Muttering under his breath, he told the crew to go around me. To go around the tree. To keep clearing, but to leave us for last. He walked away from the noise to shout into a phone for a while. After the bulldozer flattened the smaller stand of trees behind me, he returned to me and my chains.

"You have to prove this is a grave site."

"Do what?"

"Prove it. Is there documentation? A headstone? What proves that this is a place where human remains are interred?"

If my grandmother had been there, she was rich enough, and knew enough of the history of this place, she would have been able to tell him where his documentation was. If my Auntie Monica were there, she would have told him right where he could stick his documentation.

"I can't," I said, without even really trying. "But I know if you opened up this tree there would be a body inside it. Like a skeleton and stuff."

The foreman blinked slowly again. I held my breath. "Then we will open it up. If there are bones, we leave it alone."

It was as reasonable an offer I could hope to get out here by myself. The rest of my family might have been able to fight the idea, maybe get an injunction or something. But just me, by myself? I nodded.

"You'll have to un-chain yourself," the foreman pointed at my wrists.

I smiled at him, then, leaned heavily on the tree. "I can't. The key is in my jacket pocket."

With a snicker, the foreman unlocked my left-hand set of cuffs and released me from my wide hug around the tree. I dragged the chain and the right set of cuffs with me as I stepped away from the massive trunk. I'm not sure why he believed me. Or why I believed he would be good on his word, but we both trusted that this was what needed to happen. After only an hour's "stand", I backed away from my storied, beloved oak.

He took a small chainsaw and made an incision into the trunk. The engine rumbled as he pulled the screaming saw out of the wood. "It *is* hollow," He shouted to me. Duh. I knew that.

He made a few precise cuts, just enough to open a small window in the trunk of the tree. Pulling a flashlight from his belt, the man peered down into the interior space of the ancient oak. I heard him mutter "What the hell?" before he gave me a spooked look and started opening the tree in earnest.

"What the fuck do you know about this, kid?" Peering into the freshly-cut door in the tree, the guy backed up, his hands visibly shaking. The whites of his eyes showed all the way around his brown irises. He didn't look bored or angry anymore. He dropped the chainsaw as it sputtered to silence. "What the *fuck* is going on?"

I stepped forward to see what was inside the base of the hollow tree, and very nearly slipped in the spring. *Holy Shit.* The outline of a man's body was clear in the dim light, but it was not desiccated. It was not dusty remains of clothing over dried-out bones, but a real, flesh and blood man. A man who appeared to be alive – or at least recently so.

"Holy shit!" I said the words out loud as I leaned forward to touch the sleeping man covered in dust. As his face came further into view in the fading afternoon light, I realized that he could be one of my uncles, the family resemblance was so strong.

"Don't touch him!" The foreman yanked my arm, pulling me away from the man and the tree. "This is a crime scene. Don't you move! I've got to call…" He scooped up his chainsaw defensively and sidled a few feet away to get a signal.

"He's not dead." I knew. I knew it in my bones. He wasn't dead, he had been *imprisoned*. Bespelled and imprisoned. "*And in the hollow oak he lay as dead and lost to life and use and name and fame.*" I whispered the Tennyson lines. *As* dead. Not dead. Tennyson got the tree right, but the place wrong. He said that the charm couldn't be undone – had he gotten that wrong as well?

Not everyone in my family took our magical heritage seriously. Mum was a skeptic. Auntie Monica was a believer. Until a few years ago, she'd passed on everything she'd learned to me. The trickle of the stream beside the tree was not enough running water to break a spell. It was barely enough to rinse a crystal in. What else broke spells? Salt. I didn't have any salt on me. I looked around the decimated hillside. It was slick with mud and deep tracks. The splintered remains of the trees looked like a battlefield. Battlefield. Blood. Blood bound spells, but it could also break them.

I looked at the foreman where he stood on the phone with 999, eyeing me. According to our family legend, this was my forefather. My ancestor. My blood and his should – what? Recognize each other? Resonate? What the fuck was I doing?

Not thinking, and knowing I didn't have time, I pulled my pocketknife out and slashed across my inner arm, just above the wrist. I didn't look at the scars the slice of the blade was crossing. Now was not the time to think about that. I had a Grandad to rescue. I reached my arm into the tree and held my forearm high above Merlin's head. (It had to be Merlin, right? Who the hell else would it be?) as the blood dropped, dark in the dingy blackness of the hollow tree, I decided to say something. To, like, make it spellier.

"Blood to blood calls." I stammered as the liquid flowed from my arm. "Blood to blood calls, and wakes the sleeping wizard. I break the charm with Vivien's voice and Merlin's blood."

The foreman yanked me from the tree. "What the fuck do you think you're doing?"

He leaned forward to see what I'd done inside the tree, and then fell back, scrambling away from it. His face had turned a strange shade of grey. His expression seemed to be locked in a silent scream, eyes riveted on the interior of the tree.

I took off my jacket and wrapped the sleeve tight around the cut tying it in a big bright pink wad around my arm. "It's just some blood," I said to the guy.

He shook his head and waved a hand toward the tree, still backing away.

I leaned forward, peering into the darkness, and met the steely blue gaze of a very much alive and very much awake wizard.

He reached up and felt the blood dripping on his long hair. The color of the strands was hidden under the dark black-brown dirt from the interior of the oak. He looked at the blood on his fingers, then at me. I waved the ball of pink jacket around my arm in response. He nodded a little in recognition that the blood wasn't his, then took a look at his surroundings. I watched as he felt around the base of the tree, sifting through the dust and the dirt in the darkness. Finding nothing, he started to stand up.

"*Helpwch fi isefyll.*" The blinking wizard in the tree coughed a little between words. "*Helpwch fi ifyndallano'r fan hyn.*" He reached a hand toward me. A thick ring glinted on his finger.

"I don't speak that language." I said helpfully, as I reached into the tree to offer him my hand. His joints were clearly stiff. I winced to think of a thousand-year crick in my neck. He accepted my hand to help him out of the tree. It was slow going. He had been seated with knees curled to chest, and unbending knees and hips took a long time, especially with atrophied muscles.

The foreman burbled something in growing panic as Merlin squeezed his way out of the crack in the tree trunk. The clothes that had dusted his form before fell away into disintegrated drifts as he stepped from the trunk. Even his boots had decayed over the centuries.

I remembered Tennyson again. I'd never met a person to whom his skin *"clung but to crate and basket, ribs and spine."* He motioned to me, then pointed from me to the bottom of the tree. *"Helpwch ficaelfymhethau."*

I was good enough at charades to figure he wanted me to look for his belongings. I was pretty sure Vivien had stripped him clean before she imprisoned him. But I leaned forward and scrabbled through the dirt and filth at the bottom of the tree to see if I could find anything. While I fished around in the darkness, and the foreman quietly shat himself behind us, Merlin splashed around using the stream to rinse the centuries of grime off his face and arms.

I found a big round rock, a short, rusty dagger, and a clattering handful of crystals. When I turned around, the foreman was gone. I could hear automobile engines and voices at the bottom of the hill. A very bad sign. Merlin looked like a wild man. His shoulder-length hair was clumped with dirt and water, bushy eyebrows dripping water onto his sharp cheekbones. When he smiled at the sight of his belongings, his teeth were startlingly white but weirdly ground down, like short stumps. He took the big rock in his hand and rinsed it off in the stream.

"Dod o hydiffonfawr," he said. He looked at me, then motioned to a space above his own head, a little more than 2 meters. *"Am y talhwn."*

"Still don't speak that language," I told him.

He rolled his eyes and grunted. *"Ffon!"* He shouted the word and patted the tree trunk. *"Ffon!"* He repeated. Then picked up a twig. He shook the twig at me, then held the big rock, which gleamed and glittered in the sunlight after its bath. He held the rock at the height longer than 2 meters over his head again. Then made crackling weird noises that I'm not sure whether they were sound effects or words. But I got the gist.

"Brysiwch." He said the word while gazing down the hill at the approaching voices.

The wreckage of the forest was all around us. The battlefield image was still apt. Stumps stuck up at odd angles, wood and leaves littered the muddy ground like blood. It was not terribly difficult to locate a 2-meter-long branch in the mess.

I brought him the stick, and noticed he'd been washing up more. His skin was pink with the cold water and the chilly air. He wasn't old. Not like you picture Merlin. But I guess if he lived in an era when most people died by forty, a man in his mid-fifties was rare. His hair wasn't even all the way white. A good bit of brown still sprinkled throughout it. Maybe that was just dirt.

"Swydddda, blenty." He grunted as he took the stick from me. He inspected the bough, weighing the glittering rock in his hand. *"Digwyddcaelrhywfaint o linyn?"* He tapped the rock on the end of the branch as he asked the question. The rock was intended to be at the top of a stick. No, not a stick. A staff. He's a freaking wizard. How could I be so dumb?

I took off the leather necklace that I always wore. The little strap of soft black leather was probably enough to tie the rock into place. Before I could slide the charms off the strap, he pulled the necklace from my grasp.

"Diolch. Bydd y rheini'nhelpu."

Wizard charades was not going to cut it. We needed a better way to communicate. The police and A&E were making their way up the hill with the foreman weaving beside them like he was drunk. Merlin was quick at using my necklace to tie the big rock – crystal? – to the staff.

"Dda," he said, with satisfaction. He looked at me, then at the people coming up the hill. I was getting nervous about facing them, my eyes had to be as big as saucers.

He held out a hand, palm up, like he had when sitting in the tree. *"Cymrydfyllaw."*

Not knowing what else to do, I took his hand and held it. He smiled at me with his stubby teeth and spoke one blazing word. The word squeezed my skull and released it a few times, incomprehensible and vibrating. When my skull stopped jiggling, I opened my eyes to find myself still holding Merlin's hand. He wiggled his eyebrows at me, then motioned toward the fading sunlight.

We were standing on a ridge full of grasses and wildflowers one knoll away from his oak. We were still on the estate property. Still close enough to my car. But as far as the A&E crew were concerned, we had disappeared. The battleground of the forest looked like a sad, poorly shaved knob from where we stood.

Without releasing my hand, the old man said a new word. This word ground and slid like limestone working its way around bones.

"Please tell me you can understand me now." His voice was the same, but the words were a crisp modern English, accented very much like my own family's.

I sighed with relief. "Oh goodness, yes! How did you –" His scowl stopped me short.

"You are a mage, and would ask another how he does his work?"

"I'm not really a –"

"Of course you are, or would not know where to find me, or how to wake me." He dropped my hand and uttered a third word. This one spun and billowed, swirled in the grass. His conjured clothes looked like the ones the foreman had been wearing. Muddy jeans, work boots, a collared, long-sleeved shirt and a bright orange safety vest. Fully dressed, and surveying the hill, he stopped for a moment before speaking to me again.

"Are we friends, or foes, mage?"

"We're – we're family."

He grunted. "Ah, could go either way then." He started walking down the hill. "Where is the closest meal? I'm starving."

I pointed to my car, hidden in a small clutch of bushes at the bottom of the hill. It was a third-hand beast with a fourth-hand paint job of chipping primer and rusted spots around the dented fenders. But it ran. I had to dig all of Merlin's belongings out of my pockets to reach my car keys, which he happily accepted. I didn't know why he held onto them in his hands, instead of putting them in his own pockets. Unlocking the passenger-side door, I showed him how to get into the bucket seat, and how to fasten his safety belt.

He jumped when I sparked the engine and looked at me with wide eyes.

"Horseless carriage? Er. Wagon?" I said, hoping that made sense to him. He grumbled something and shook his head but did not protest when I put the car into gear and backed onto the narrow country road.

"Your wagon travels very fast, but it is noisy." He said, gripping the door with one hand and his lap belt with the other.

"Would you like me to slow down?"

"No. Food is more important." He shivered a little. "And real clothing. These are an illusion." I turned on the heater full blast, hoping that would help him feel better.

I didn't dare take him to a restaurant, though they would be able to help him more than my meager kitchen would. The police and A&E back at the oak may put out a radio call to look for a strange, filthy man who'd woken up in a tree. I was a little worried we'd still be caught.

My kitchen it was.

My flat was a converted attic above a garage in the bad part of town. I didn't like the perpetual smell of petrol, or the lack of a proper door, but my landlady let me keep my own car inside the garage. He followed me up the stairs to the tiny space I called home. Aside from a small loo in one corner, it was a single shabby room hung with tie-dye bedsheets to cover up the pink fiberglass insulation. A curtain of cloudy PVC plastic sheeting separated my room from the garage below, but mostly it just kept the attic from heating too much of the garage.

I decided that a frozen pizza was as good as any first meal after however many hundreds of years of being in a tree, and preheated the oven while Merlin met my cat.

"What's his name?" the man asked, bending down to stroke the blue-black fur of the massive feline that had adopted me.

"Merlin." I nearly choked.

"No, *his* name." Merlin smiled at me with those short teeth. He stroked the cat's long back. "A worthy namesake."

"The food is going to take a few minutes to prepare." I moved stuff around in the tiny bathroom to create space, sniffing towels to find my guest a clean one. "If you want to take a shower – er, bathe?"

Rising from the cat with more grace and speed than I expected, Merlin followed me into the tiny space. I awkwardly showed him the various knobs of the shower and tub, then backed away. He had already dropped the illusion of the workman's clothes. I grabbed the first aid kit and jumped out of the little room.

My jacket was ruined. But the cut had scabbed over. It wasn't deep. I cleaned it without picking the scab and then wrapped it with bandages to keep anyone who might see me from worrying. The oven beeped, ready for the frozen slab of meat and cheese, and I realized the next step would be finding clothing that would be suitable for Merlin. And that might not trigger a call to any authorities about a strange not-dead man trapped in a tree.

My closet was not helpful. Since I'd moved out and came out, I had transitioned all my clothes as best I could. I mean, thrift shops and consignment boutiques couldn't really do it justice, but it was better than the clothes that made me feel like a giant imposter. My eyes landed on the cardboard box in the closet floor. It was duct-taped closed and intended to be burned or given away or at least never opened by me again. But. Merlin was not that much taller than me, and he was skin and bones. Some of those clothes might fit him.

By the time the pizza was ready, the wizard emerged from the bathroom in a plume of steam. "Is that food? It smells wonderful!"

Imagine only ever eaten roast meat or stew, only things that are hearty and old fashioned like shepherd's pie or blood pudding. Imagine being served your first slice of pepperoni pizza in your mid-fifties. Imagine it being the first thing you've eaten in a thousand years.

He burned the roof of his mouth on the cheese. He burned his lips on the sauce. He did not care. I didn't dare ask him if I could have a slice. I did, eventually, get him a small glass of water.

"You *are* a mage." He said the words with satisfaction as he finished the last bite of crust and nibbled globs of melted cheese off his plate. "Tell me, what should I call you?"

"Gwen," I smiled at the old wizard as I told him my name.

"Thank you for freeing me, Gwen." He said the words gravely, looking me in the eyes as he did it. "Now, how exactly are you and I family?"

"My grandmother would be able to explain it better." I slashed through the duct tape on the box of clothes. "But according to our family legend, we are direct descendants of the child that Vivien conceived with you right before she shut you in that tree."

"Descendants. Grandchildren?"

"Many times removed. It's been – at least?-- a thousand years." I recoiled at the blue suit. The suit for weddings, funerals, and job interviews. It was the worst of the items in the box. The most required. The biggest lie.

Merlin grunted at my suggestion of the timeline and decided to ignore it. Instead, he turned his attention to the box of clothes I was unpacking. He took a pair of cargo pocketed khaki pants and shook them out. They made me feel like a lesbian when I wore them. He tried them on, and though they were a little large around the waist, they did the job. I tossed him a blue button-collared shirt to try with them. He put his crystals in the cargo pocket of the pants and grinned at me.

"You can have all this," I said, still pulling clothes out of the box. "Any of it you want." I pulled a slim khaki canvas belt from my closet and tried it around his waist.

"I would like to discuss your family with your grandmother." He said the words as if he knew I wouldn't like hearing them. I didn't.

There were a pair of black loafers at the bottom of the box that were too expensive to throw away, and too masculine to wear. I put them beside his feet, trying to decide whether they would be too large for him or not.

"Why do you have a box of men's clothing? Did you kill this man?

Did you seduce him?" Merlin was half asking me, and half muttering to his knees as he pulled socks and shoes on.

"They were mine, before—"

"Before what?"

"Before I transitioned."

"You transformed yourself from a man into a woman?"

"I was always a woman," I sighed, not sure how the hell I was going to explain this to a centuries-old wizard. "I was born a woman. But everyone thought I was a man. When I transitioned, I stopped pretending to be a man."

"You were born cursed, and finally dispelled the glamour." The dude nodded at me as if this made total sense to him. "Not the first I've known."

I DIDN'T WANT to see my grandmother. After no one showed up at the tree, I wasn't sure I wanted to see anyone in my family. But Merlin deserved whatever answers they could give him.

We waited until the following morning before we drove across the hills to the large estate house where my grandmother lived. Her land had been disconnected from the hills where the tree had grown several hundred years ago, but it was supposed to be undeveloped park land. The people who bought the park for a housing development had found a loophole in the will. My little car spluttered along the narrow lanes and Merlin sank into the passenger seat.

"Doing okay?" I asked him after I spotted how white his face had become.

"It's nauseating, this wagon."

I eased my foot off the accelerator. Between the winding, bumpy road and the speed, this part of the country would make anyone a little green at the gills, even if you were used to cars.

Merlin didn't say anything when we pulled up to my grandmother's mansion. He didn't say anything as he followed me up the wide marble steps to the front door. Or when the butler opened the massive black maw of the house.

"Hi James," I said with a sheepish smile. "I need to see my grandmother."

James raised his eyebrows at both me and my companion, but he stepped aside silently, motioning for us to enter the house. I didn't wait for him to make us welcome, or not, I just turned an immediate left into the music room. It had always been my favorite room in the old house, and I wasn't going to pass up a chance to visit it. James blinked at me, then nodded, and went to find my grandmother and alert her of her guests.

Merlin touched each instrument in the room in turn. He plucked a string on the huge standing harp, then one on the cello. He placed his fingers on the piano keys with a discordant bleat of sound. Jumping back and smiling at me like a kid, he asked "Do you know how to use these?"

I walked over to the baby grand and placed my fingertips along the center of the keys. I played a few scales to get the muscle memory going, then spread my fingers and played a big, bold chord. Grinning up at the delighted Merlin, I played a little bit of a sad Beethoven concerto – the only thing I could still play from memory. When my memory failed me, and my fingers slowed upon the keys, he clapped his hands.

"Good morning, XXXXXX." My grandmother's voice was icy in the threshold. I shuddered at my deadname as I turned to face her.

"Good morning, grandmother. Please call me Gwen." I squared my shoulders and swallowed.

"Your mother named you." She said the words with crisp finality as she entered the room and perched on one of the lounges. "Who is your companion?"

I took a deep breath. Before I could get the story out – about the tree, about Merlin – about any of it, he stepped forward and bowed with true courtly manner.

"My lady," he said, facing the carpet at his feet, "I believe we are members of the same family. My name is Myrddn Emerys. Though most of my friends call me simply Merlin." The smile he gave her was dashing enough that I nearly fluttered my eyelashes at it.

My grandmother rolled her eyes and looked at me. "Is this supposed to be a joke?"

Again, I opened my mouth to speak, and Merlin beat me to it. "Why would anyone joke about such a serious matter?"

"XXXXXX is obsessed with –"

"I'm sorry, I do not know anyone by the name of XXXXXX in this place. Do you mean Gwen?"

"XXXXXX." My grandmother spat my deadname. "*He* is obsessed with the tales of our –"

Merlin stood up abruptly. His expression reminded me of the Tennyson line.

He dragged his eyebrow bushes down, and made
A snowy penthouse for his hollow eyes.

His eyebrows were more salt and pepper than snowy, but it was still an apt description.

"Gwen, is she the one who cursed you?" Merlin's gaze darted between my grandmother's scowl and my shocked face. "Do I need to kill her?"

Grandmother clutched a hand to her heart.

"No!" I jumped forward. Standing between Merlin and grandmother, I turned to her. "This man needs to know how we are related to Merlin. It's about the oak tree." I lied without lying.

"The oak tree." She scoffed. "The tree that you so foolishly attempted to save yesterday?"

Merlin glanced at me and then at her. "Gwen. We'll get no answers here." His eyebrows were still a bushy penthouse for his eyes. He took my hand, and with a straight spine, led me back to the front door.

Just as his hand pressed the thick silver knob, my grandmother called back to us, "Did you save the tree?" Her voice held a tremor of hope and concern. But just a tremor.

Merlin turned to face her, bearing his full scowl. "No, the tree is gone. But she saved me from inside it."

Leaving my grandmother with her mouth agape, we returned to my car under the thundercloud of Merlin's eyebrows. "There has to be someone else."

I put the car into gear and punched Monica's address into my GPS. "My aunt won't be much better." I warned him. "And I guarantee my grandmother is calling her right now."

"What of your parents?" He looked at me, still frowning.

I shook my head a little. What was the use? They would deadname me and purposely misgender me. They would treat Merlin like he was some madman and not an ancient wizard. *And* they wouldn't have any information.

Still clutching his seatbelt and the handle of the door beside him, Merlin gazed out the windscreen to master his nausea.

"I have an idea," he said, as we pulled into my aunt's driveway.

"Okay." His idea might be awful. But it was better than my lack of ideas.

He pulled his staff out of the space between our seats. Getting out of the car, he spoke one of the words he had the day before. The one that spun and billowed, the one that swirled. His clothes changed into a series of furs and robes, a dangling leather pouch at his waist beside a dagger. His clean-shaven chin grew a long, white beard. And his relatively short hair grew to his shoulders, steel grey with shots of brown and white.

"How do I look?" He asked, stroking his glamour beard.

I grinned. He looked like a LARPer playing a wizard. He was only missing the pointy hat and small wire-rimmed glasses. He winked at me, and then led the way to Auntie Monica's front step.

She wrenched the door open before we could knock on the door. Her black hair was frizzy and falling out of a bun. She was wearing a T-shirt and yoga pants. "Didn't your mother teach you to call before visiting people, XXXXXX? You know better."

"I apologize for our intrusion, my lady." Merlin did his courtly bow thing. "It is due to my urgency that my young friend was not able to call."

His "young friend." He could manage to keep my gender right, even when talking to my family. My heart ached with it. My umpty-great-grandfather was the only family I had. He was an ancient wizard and I loved him.

Monica responded to the manners with a blush and a smile, but she eyed the LARPing wizard with more than a little suspicion. "And you are?"

"My lady, that is the mystery we require your help with!" His most winning, dazzling smile seemed to have charmed my aunt. With an odd little tilt of her head, she swung the door wide and allowed us to enter.

As we walked into her front room, Merlin's eyes landed upon her various pagan knickknacks and magickal paraphernalia. One curling white eyebrow hair twitched as he noticed sigils on the wall.

"You are a mage, my lady." He said the words gravely, without question. Aunt Monica glanced from Merlin to me.

"She taught me everything I know," I said. The tension in the room didn't decrease like I'd hoped it would.

"Cut to the chase," Monica said. She backed into the room to take a seat in her tallest velvet chair.

"I went to the knoll to save the oak tree yesterday, like I said." I wrung my hands and tried not to draw attention to my bandaged arm. Merlin sat down across the room from Aunt Monica. Neither of them looked at me. "I told the foreman that it was a grave and they couldn't defile it. Since I didn't have paperwork or anything…"

I tried to keep my voice calm. I wanted to be snarky about it. *Since I was doing it by myself.* Monica had disappointed me the most when she hadn't shown up. "He wanted me to prove it was a grave. So, he opened up the tree to see if there were bones inside."

"They opened up the oak tree?" Monica's mouth dropped open a little. She looked at me for the first time.

"The foreman got really spooked when there weren't bones inside the tree, but a whole person. A not-dead person. He called the police."

"What do you mean a person?" Monica's eyes narrowed.

"There was a living person sleeping inside the tree. Remember

Tennyson? *'And in the hollow oak he lay as dead, and lost to life and use and name and fame'*." I looked my favorite aunt in the eye. "He was bespelled, not killed." I glanced at Merlin, but he seemed content to let me continue talking. "Anyway, while the foreman was ringing the police, I figured out how to break the spell. The stream didn't have enough running water. I didn't have salt or anything. So I tried blood." I held up my bandaged arm. "It worked."

Monica's face went through a series of expressions: confusion, distress, anger, disbelief, wonder, suspicion. "You expect me to believe this?"

Merlin smiled a little where he sat. He thumped his staff on the floor and dropped the hokey glamour. Sitting there in my old clothes, he looked like a tired uncle, not a wizard. She jumped at the minor trick. He said a word. This word made the room collapse into my belly button and expand inside my knees. I wanted to sneeze. When the sensation passed, the hairs on the back of my neck stood up. He was a giant black wolf. Sitting in Monica's front room. He walked forward, gave her a big slobbery lick across the face, then transformed back into tired uncle vibes.

"We do, my lady, ask you to believe this."

Wiping the wolf drool off her face, Monica winced, then shook her head. "Okay, fine. Why are you here?"

"Merlin would like to know better how we're related. I don't know the history stuff as well as you do –"

"You should ask Mother, she knows –"

"She did not believe us." Merlin looked abashed. "We did not impress upon her the truth of our situation." The image of Merlin transforming himself into a wolf in my grandmother's music room flashed through my mind. I choked on a giggle.

Monica blinked at the sound I made. She blinked at Merlin. She blinked at me again, and then nodded. "Okay."

She went to the locked cabinet at the far end of the room. Taking a small key from her charm bracelet, she popped the solid doors open, and pulled out three large, leather-bound books full of irregularly shaped pieces of vellum, parchment, and homemade paper. The books made a dusty thump on the coffee table as she piled them before Merlin and me. She then drew a metal lockbox from the bottom shelf of the cabinet. Using a second key from her charm bracelet, she opened that one. She then dusted it with a feather and whispered a few words.

She placed that box in front of Merlin as well. Then, as if she were challenging him, she sat down in her chair and faced him without another word. He bowed graciously toward her, and with a brief glance at me, he opened the metal box.

The box was lined with black velvet and cushions, as if what it protected was very rare and very valuable. In the center of the lining was another container. Merlin turned the cube over in his hand curiously. Beneath the cube rested a plastic bag containing gloves and long tweezers.

"It's an archival chamber," Monica said. "It's intended to keep moisture in the air sealed away from what's inside, so it doesn't rot or disintegrate." She pointed at the bag. "Put on the gloves, and I'll show you how to open it. We can't touch it with our fingers, or we'll introduce oil and potential decay."

Merlin drew on the gloves obediently and followed her careful instructions for the container. It opened with the pop and hiss of vacuum-sealed air. Inside the container, cushioned in more padding, was a small book made of very old leather. Merlin's breath hitched when he saw it. Recognizing its fragility and value, he rested the book on the archival container and used the tweezers and gloved fingertips to reverently, slowly, examine the pages.

Lord Tennyson popped into my mind unbidden.

It is but twenty pages long,
But every page having an ample marge,
And every marge enclosing in the midst
A square of text that looks a little blot,
The text no larger than the limbs of fleas;
And every square of text an awful charm,
Writ in a language that has long gone by.

I SAID the words out loud. Merlin ignored me. Monica barely glanced at me. Family legend whispered of some Victorian great-great-aunt who let the poet sneak a peep at the precious book that Vivian stole from Merlin. How else could he have described it so well?

And every margin scribbled, crost, and crammed
With comment, densest condensation, hard
To mind and eye; but the long sleepless nights
Of my long life have made it easy to me.
And none can read the text, not even I;
And none can read the comment but myself..."

"Can you read it?" Monica asked as my voice hung in the silence.

Merlin smiled a little. "Some. Not all. It was never meant to be read. Not really." He placed the book gently back among its cushions. "Can you?"

Monica returned his smile. "I deciphered one word. A few of our ancestors have had better luck. We – we have been trying to translate it." She motioned toward the dusty heap of books from within the locked box.

The skin around Merlin's eyes crinkled. The grey-blue irises glinted. "One word. What did it teach you?"

Monica looked into his eyes for several moments. My aunt had gone pale and still as she stared at the wizard. "It was... awful." Her voice caught in her throat.

Merlin watched her face reflect the horror she had witnessed. "These words are not meant to be spoken lightly." His voice was gentle and low. "Do you regret it?"

"I—" She looked at her hands. "I don't regret the time I have spent with the book. I regret speaking the word."

"Time spent with the book..." Merlin turned the small item over in his hands. "This is the work of lifetimes. More lifetimes than you or I could imagine. And more deaths than either of us can conceive of." Merlin gestured toward me with the small object. "Gwen knows that it was my undoing." He placed it back in the little box, carefully replacing the gloves and tweezers. "Be careful how much time you pay attention to it. It will take as much as it gives."

He replaced the box and pressed his hands away from himself. An act of refusal and benediction. If Aunt Monica thought he was going to request his belongings back, she pretended to be unsurprised when he did not.

She drew one of the leather-bound books from the dusty stack. Opening the yellow pages to the beginning, she showed him the thin cursive script that listed names and dates and more names and dates. "Here is the lineage."

Merlin looked at the names and flicked through the pages with a soft exhale. "How many generations?" he asked. His eyes gleamed a little in the dim light. I could see the years that he had spent enclosed in a tree sink into his face. It was as if the gentle hairline wrinkles deepened by millimeters with each generation on the page. It started to sink in. How long he had been asleep. How far he was from home. How long-dead his friends really were. He opened the book back to the beginning. "I sired a daughter. A daughter I never met." His voice was nearly inaudible.

His fingers turned page after page as the script changed and the pages grew less yellow deeper in the book. Uncomfortable, Monica returned to her cupboard and withdrew a small piece of jewelry. It was a hair stick, but shaped like a golden snake, coiled and ready to strike.

"Legend says this belonged to her," Monica said, interrupting Merlin's sorrow.

He glanced up, and a small huff of air snorted from his nose. She held it out, but he refused to touch it. "Yes, that looks like hers. A viper she always was. With hair as dark as yours, and a mouth as lovely as fair Gwen's."

Before she could deadname me, he snapped the genealogy book closed. "Thank you, dear lady, for your time." He said, recovering his previous bravado. "We'll be going now, Gwen?"

∾

MERLIN WAS silent in the car ride back to my apartment. I had thought about taking him out for curry, but he didn't seem to be in the mood for new cuisine. Though I was having a hard time figuring out what kind of mood he was in. His face was expressionless. Even his eyebrows were relaxed, or at least they seemed to be until we both saw the police officer standing in the driveway in front of my small garage and flat.

"Authority?" He said, eyeing the posture of the man. "A knight of some sort?"

"Kind of." I nodded. "We call police officers like him when someone breaks the law. And they capture the person."

"Officer is his title?"

"Yes."

Merlin nodded a little to himself and got out of the car before I'd even stopped the engine.

"Hello, officer! Can we help you?" The wizard had become a genial version of the tired uncle guise more quickly than I could have imagined. His adaptability made it easy to forget that he was thousands of years old.

"Hi – er, sir?" The officer looked at a slip of paper in his hand. "I'm looking for a Mr. Emerson. Rents this flat."

Merlin turned to me and gave me a puzzled look. "My daughter Gwen stays in this flat." When he called me his daughter something warm and bright burned in my belly. "Gwen, do you know anyone named Emerson?"

I keyed the garage door opener, offering to let the policeman step inside out of the wind. "I sublet from that guy, Dad. He was quiet. Seemed a little odd." The word "dad" tripped off my tongue in the improv of the moment, but Merlin and I met gazes as I said it.

"I'm sorry for this intrusion, miss." The officer nodded and walked toward his car. "Do you have any contact information for Mr. Emerson?"

"Afraid not. I have all the information for the landlady. I pay fees directly to her."

"Is the lad in trouble?" Merlin asked, leaning forward. "Did he do something wrong? If he has keys to my Gwennie's flat..." His voice lowered protectively. I nearly swooned. *My Gwennie.*

The officer shook his head and looked at his notebook. "No, no, he's not dangerous. We're just tying up some loose ends on a strange incident over in the hills yesterday. We thought he might be able to fill in some gaps for us." The police officer flipped the cover of the notebook closed and tucked it into a pocket. "Unnecessary paper-work, really. It's not like it was a crime scene. A hoax, most likely. Thank you for your time, Mister and Miss... er?" He trailed off, not knowing our last name.

"Emrys." Merlin smiled. "Old Welsh name."

"Thank you for your time, Mister Emrys, Miss Emrys. Please let us know if you hear from XXXXXX."

"Thank you, officer, we will." I nearly burst out giggling before the officer closed the door on his car.

Merlin and I looked at each other. I had eyes not so very different from his grey-blue ones. "Father, huh?"

He shrugged and blushed a little. "I figure the rest of the family for enemies, Gwennie. They want to keep you cursed. And I never met my first daughter."

20

A BIRD FOR A BIRD

The birds had gone silent, and thunderclouds loomed over the bridal party, menacing the ceremony with the threat of rain. I glanced up at the sky but tried to keep my eyes trained on my sister Lisbeth, the bride. Frankly, anything was better than meeting the glittering black eyes of the groom.

Fitcher was our brother-in-law already, or he had been. He had married our eldest sister a year previous. He claims that she had fallen violently ill and that the authorities would not let us tend her body for fear of contagion. He gave us an urn with her ashes instead. My dead sister's husband was back, ready to marry Lissy, our middle sister. He made me feel strange things when he met my gaze. Warm, liquid, feminine feelings in the lower part of my body paradoxically amplified the curdling, cowering instincts in my belly. It was like a human version of the simultaneous repulsion and attraction so many of us have for gory horror films.

He was wealthy. Moderately charming. Ate at fine restaurants and hobnobbed with celebrities. That had to be the reason why Lisbeth would agree, after losing her sister, to marrying this man. He owned a literal estate out past the dark forest, with one of those mansions that would occasionally get featured in magazines. I didn't know why we were holding this ceremony in our small, suburban backyard, rather than on the sweeping lawns of his giant house. Lissy never told me.

Thunder clapped on the other side of town during their vows. We couldn't hear them promise to protect and love and obey, though I assumed the minister could hear them. That was his job after all.

Lightning flashed less than a mile away and the leaves turned upside down on all the trees lining our small yard. The storm was coming fast. The perfunctory ceremony was faster. Like the last wedding, Fitcher had no friends or family in attendance. He had a dude there who I swear was a butler. No family, no fancy friends to protect from the rain. Lisbeth was tucked into the back of the limo before the first fat droplets fell from the sky. She was gone before we could get the minister into the kitchen out of the rain.

A sense of dread had settled into my stomach.

"SURELY YOU HAVE TAKEN a wrong turn, young lady." The stilted accent and affected tones of the voice over my shoulder alerted me to be polite. I smiled and lowered my gaze as I turned.

"The party was too much for me," I admitted. "I needed to take a break." I feigned lightness of head and weakness of body. The woman patted me on the hand. She was older than my mother, wearing a glittering crystal blue gown.

"I understand," she said, gripping my wrist with a firmer grasp than I anticipated her having. "But this area of the house is private, and guests should be closer to the ballroom." The ring on her index finger was massive and cobalt blue. I wasn't sure if it was glass or something else. I knew this bookshelf-lined study meant something – something about it called to me. But this woman had taken it upon herself to be the party police and was firmly and stubbornly dragging me to the door.

"Perhaps a trip to the powder room will help," she offered, steering us toward the large powder room that had been designated for female guests, complete with fainting couches.

Lisbeth was nowhere to be seen. She'd begged me to agree to attend this party. She'd sent me dress after dress to try on so I'd fit in. She just wanted one familiar face here, she'd said.

But she didn't greet me when I arrived, and I wasn't sure Fitcher even knew I was there. I had been hunting through the house as best I could to locate her. It wasn't like Lissy to miss a chance to meet movie stars. I decided to see if my "guide" could help. "Have you seen the lady of the house tonight?" I asked her.

Her grip tensed a small bit on my arm, and her lips pressed together. "No," the woman replied. "No, I have not."

"I'm here at her invitation," I pressed on. "I'd really like to see her."

The hand on my wrist felt like a talon. It was as if a harpy was dragging me to the crowded powder room. "I hadn't realized she had invited anyone," the woman said with a frown. I had been on the verge of introducing myself to the woman as Lissy's sister, but something told me to forbear.

The woman deposited me on a fainting couch and promptly deserted me. I paused there for a breath, then discreetly followed her. The glittering white-blue of her gown was easy to spot as she made a slice through the mingling crowd like a knife. I watched as my brother-in-law's dark head tilted toward her. In the next moment, his gaze met mine.

My stomach dropped. *Fuck.*

I nabbed a champagne flute off a passing tray and spun to smile at the next guest. He was a young fashion icon. A recent science fiction film had rocketed him to superstardom. I didn't remember his name. I barely heard his words, though I vaguely got the impression he was flirting with me. All that I could concentrate on was the thundering of my heartbeat and the mental JAWS theme as my sisters' husband slowly edged across the room toward me.

"Robin, dear sister, so kind of you to join us this evening." I could feel his breath on my left shoulder. The science fiction superstar smiled at his host and then wandered off, dismissed and bewildered.

I turned slowly, pretending to be genteel, trying to keep the visible shaking to a minimum. This man had always given me the creeps. Now, his creepiness had turned up the volume. He was tall, maybe 6'2" or 6'3" and had flowing dark brown hair to his shoulders like a rock star. There were a few strands of silver at each temple, just enough to make him look adult, but not old. He reminded me of Gary Oldman in that 90s version of Dracula. Just needed the old-timey outfits and Winona Ryder.

I needed a Keanu. And my little science fiction fella had given up so quickly.

"Thank you for having me," I finally said around a tongue too thick on anxiety.

My skin crawled as his gaze groped its way up the front of my body. "You look wonderful." I regretted the plunging vee of my neckline and the hint of cleavage presented by the black dress. I regretted the clinging silk fabric. Then, following the pause of his gaze, I also regretted not covering up my tattoo, as Lissy had advised me to do.

It's small, maybe four inches. A little red breasted robin perched on an antique skeleton key, a ladybug jutting from its beak. It sits on my collarbone above my left breast. The wide halter straps of the dress concealed most of it. Just the bird's head and its little prey poked out.

"A bird for a bird." He murmured.

"I can't seem to locate Lissy anywhere?" I asked the question directly. No sense in pretending I was there for any other reason.

"Your sister is indisposed this evening." He said the words as if he was very sad about the fact indeed.

"She wouldn't miss this for the world," I motioned toward the hobnobbing throng of A-listers near the ice sculptures.

"She is very upset that she had to miss the party." He tilted his head at me. "Why don't you join me? Play the hostess?" He held out his right elbow as if I were supposed to naturally accept such a preposterous proposal.

"If she's ill, I should go upstairs and see her. Take her some soup or something."

He dropped his elbow, but not the overly nice façade. "I'm afraid that's not possible. She's not here."

"Not here? Is she at the hospital?"

"No, no, nothing like that. She's merely very contagious, and she didn't want to accidentally infect a houseful of guests." He paused, thinking. "That's probably why she didn't let you know. Didn't want to spoil the party for you."

"She knew I wouldn't come if she weren't here."

"Exactly. And she wanted you to enjoy yourself."

He was lying. His eyes darted around the room. His shoulders stayed low and relaxed, but his tone of voice had constricted. He wanted to be anywhere but standing beside me answering questions about Lissy.

Suddenly, his offer to play hostess appealed to me after all.

~

MY MOTHER STARED at the urn of ashes with a cold, dead gaze.

"He killed them." I told her. There was no doubt in my mind. "He killed Emily. And he killed Lissy."

"He needs to get that house inspected for black mold or something." Mom didn't seem to hear my words. She was sitting at the kitchen table, a cold mug of coffee and unbuttered toast between her hands and the urn.

"Black mold isn't a contagious infection," I said. "And these probably aren't even her ashes. He killed them both."

The more I heard my own voice say the words out loud, the more certain I was. This time, they penetrated my mom's grief.

"He's going to come for you next, Robin." She knew. She knew as well as I did. Not only had Fitcher killed both of my older sisters, but he wanted to make it a complete set.

~

I wasn't one of those True Crime girls. I didn't watch CSI and listen to murder podcasts like some of my friends did. But I guess I still had enough Nancy Drew and Scooby Doo in my blood to make me accept Fitcher's invitation for dinner. I wanted to know what happened to my sisters. If he wanted a complete set of the three of us, then this was really my opportunity.

The restaurant was small and quiet. The courses were plated like sculptures and totaled one delectable bite each. We were tucked in the corner of a patio on moderately uncomfortable iron furniture. In the candlelight, Fitcher looked almost appealing.

I'd dressed for cleavage, since that had seemed to draw his attention at the party. It was a good call. He was distracted by my breasts. If I got uncomfortable with his relentless eye contact, I could just sigh and he'd break it.

Emily had met Fitcher at a charity gala. She was organizing the silent auction to raise money for children orphaned by cancer. He was a target account – someone who had money to burn and could use the non-profit as a tax write off. She had been instantly taken with him. She liked his money, for sure, but he was also exactly her type. Tall, dark, handsome with a hint of Heathcliff on the moors.

After he'd handed her urn of ashes over to mother, I thought we'd seen the last of him. But then a few weeks later, Lisbeth came home, flushed and breathless, after running into him in town.

That was when I started Googling mister Fitcher Barbosa. It wasn't in the press, not in national news. But when I used my ancestry.com membership, I found him in the records. Marriage and death certificates. And it wasn't just Emily. It was almost a dozen dead brides. All within a year of marrying him. All with perfectly acceptable medical causes of death. No fanfare, no big news splash. Just tragic death after tragic death.

I forced myself to smile at him as I took a sip of pinot noir.

"I'm surprised you accepted my invitation," he admitted.

"I'm surprised you invited me."

"You've never seemed to like me very much, Robin." He took the most recent course, a small filet mignon into his mouth.

I took a bite as well, mostly to buy time. I didn't like him very much.

"Of course, strong, independent women like you tend to react with anger when faced with a man you're genuinely attracted to. It shows you your weakness." He said these words seriously, as if it were the truth and not some kind of joke. I dropped my gaze to the table, and hoped my flushed face seemed like a shy confession rather than incandescent rage and incredulity. My chest felt like it was full of magma.

The tender, juicy steak was like swallowing sawdust.

"Wow."

He chuckled, pleased with the things he read into my reaction. I felt like I was going to vibrate out of my chair in horror. This man's self-concept couldn't read my expressions any way other than the way that flattered him.

I barely had to flirt to keep him interested. I just had to be there, with my cleavage exposed, and not actually throw things at him as he talked. I didn't have to interact or offer opinions. He wasn't interested in what I did for a living. In fact, he didn't ask any questions about me at all. How had Rorty described Humpbert Humbert? "A monster of incuriosity." Yes. That.

I was certain he'd behaved this way with my sisters. Emily was too insecure to notice it or do anything about it. Lissy would have noticed it and kept her mouth shut. She didn't want to marry him because he was handsome. She wanted his network. She had wanted to divorce him and marry a movie star after a torrid affair. She was flattered at his attention, and ambitious for her own fame.

Oddly, as much as he talked, I didn't know exactly how he'd amassed his fortune.

"What do you do for work, Fitcher?" I asked when he gave me a chance to speak.

"In the old days, I'd have been considered a merchant. But instead of importing wares and shipping them, I import celebrities and talents."

"You're an agent?"

"I work with agents. I get their big Australian soap star on the Hollywood A-list, or their no-name Welsh singer onto the stage at the Grammys." He got into his verbal groove. "You probably noticed how many A-listers were at my party, but there were also a handful of these imported wanna-be stars in the mix…"

HE WANTED A COURTHOUSE WEDDING. A wedding in our back yard again. Something small with no fanfare. I pushed back. I wanted a big wedding with A-listers at his house. A huge party.

We compromised by him asking me to move in and setting a later date for the wedding itself.

My mother had stopped talking with me. She knew I was doing this so I could learn about my sisters, but she wanted nothing to do with it. She wasn't ready to lose another daughter, and she wasn't going to support my need to know. She didn't help me pack or move my things.

The butler from Lissy's wedding helped me load my belongings into the back of the limo. I didn't take much. I didn't intend to stay there for long.

Windshield wipers could barely keep up with the torrential downpour we drove through. The butler drove the limo as Fitcher waxed poetic about where we could go on our honeymoon. He tried to make it sound like the trip was all romance and whatever, but he'd already slipped that New Zealand was also home of the next starlet he'd be importing.

The old woman with the crystal blue gown and the talon-hands was there waiting for us. Her name, I discovered, was Mrs. Murphy, and she ran the household at the big ass mansion.

WE DELAYED the wedding a little more. Haggling over location and cost, over the guest list. I needed time alone in that house, to look for clues as to what had happened to my sisters. Mrs. Murphy was like a shadow, haunting my every move.

While we had tentatively set a date, Fitcher had to go starlet-hunting abroad. I looked forward to spending some time in the house without him. Particularly in that study I'd wandered into during Lissy's party. He spent all his time there.

"Here are the keys to the house." Fitcher said solemnly the night before he left. "I ask only that you do not open the door that this small key accesses." It was a little gold key shaped like an old-fashioned skeleton key. I shrugged and agreed to that request. "A man must have some privacy, you see."

Then he pulled the weirdest thing out of his pocket. "And this, this is special." It was a small blue egg. It looked like a robin's egg. When he handed it to me, it was delicate and light. Strangely precious. "I can't take this with me on the plane. You must keep it safe. Keep it warm. In your hand or your bra is ideal."

"What is it?" I didn't think the answer would be an obvious one.

"It's an egg, Robin." Fitcher acted like I was stupid. But then he smirked a little and relented. "And it's magical."

I didn't believe that for a moment. But it felt special and fragile. I promised to keep it safe and warm.

I waited that night until Mrs. Murphy was asleep. I tucked the weird little blue egg safely inside my sock drawer nestled near a heating pad. Wrangling the keys as silently as I could, I crept through the house. My first stop was that creepy study.

The study smelled bad. It smelled like blood – like old menstrual pads. But it was as if Fitcher had been trying to mask the smell with cigar smoke. But there were no locks that fit small golden keys.

I wandered the rest of the house, testing keys in every locked door. The keys themselves mostly opened storage cupboards.

The basement was strange. It wasn't a place I wanted to wander in the dark. But for a house this huge, it was a very small space. I wasn't sure how I'd shake Mrs. Murphy to explore it more in daylight hours. But like the study, it felt off.

Before I went back to bed, I returned to the study once again.

Focusing on the area of the room that smelled the most like old blood, I stared at the bookshelves. There was a book with no title that was the exact shade of blue of the small egg I'd tucked away upstairs. Curious, I pulled it from the shelf with one finger. Instead of sliding toward me, it tilted. It tilted and there was a small click.

The entire bookshelf loosened itself from the wall.

Inhaling a little gasp of breath, I swung the bookshelf open. It revealed one small door. A small door with an old-fashioned golden lock. The kind of lock that would fit an old-fashioned, golden key. The little key – the one Fitcher had warned me not to use – fit in the lock perfectly. I spent one heart-pounding moment doubting that I should open the door. I should listen to him. Respect his privacy.

Fuck that. I wanted to know what happened to my sisters.

The stench when I opened the small door was overwhelming. It smelled like blood.

The door showed a small staircase leading down. Down. Ah, so that's where the rest of the basement was.

Bracing myself for whatever was smelling so horribly, I flicked on the lights and went down the small curving staircase and rounded into the scene from a horror movie. The chamber was covered in blood. A wide stone basin of blood rested in the center of the room. There were body parts hanging from hooks that lined the ceiling like a butcher's freezer. Torsos and limbs. The disembodied heads of beautiful women, their faces frozen in horror, long hair trailing down into the air like banners.

Those ashes he gave my mother were not my sisters' ashes.

I found my sisters.

Not really thinking about what I was doing, or how I'd explain my actions, I pulled Lissy's head down off the hook. Using her skin tone and the shape of the slices on her neck, I pulled down her torso. Slowly, methodically, found all of my sister Lisbeth's body parts. I solemnly reassembled her.

I nearly screamed when she suddenly gasped for air and blinked her eyes. She almost screamed as she came back to consciousness. We managed to keep one another quiet in the first crucial moments as the level of blood in the basin receded a few inches, and she stood up. Alive. We embraced, crying for a few minutes. Then, without speaking, we turned to find the parts for our eldest sister, Emily.

We only had a few hours before dawn, and we had to get the blood off of us before we went back upstairs.

"The egg." Emily said, still naked, standing in my tower bedroom. "What did you do with the egg?"

"Yeah, that's what gave me away, too." Lissy said, sitting on my bed.

"It's in my sock drawer with a heating pad." I pointed at the drawer. They pulled out the drawer, and the three of us peered down at the little blue egg.

"There's no blood on it, thank god." Emily sighed in relief.

"I had it in my bra," Lissy said, afraid to touch it. "Get cleaned up before you touch it. It stains with the blood. That's how he'll know you found us."

I had forbidden housekeeping to enter my room the moment I moved into the house, much to Mrs. Murphy's dismay. So my sisters hid there until I could figure out a way to get them out of the house and safely to our mother. I did not have to wait long for the opportunity.

Fitcher returned to the house with a starlet, and plans for another large party. The pretty brunette starlet was set up in a guest suite in the distant wing of the house. A party would get my sisters out the door rapidly. I pitched the idea of a masquerade. He hated the idea – the point was to get the starlet's face seen and known among those who need to see and know her. But the starlet was completely smitten with the idea. She swore she would wear only the tiniest of masks.

I made no such promise.

When Fitcher asked me for his keys and the magic egg back, I handed both over as if I'd spent the whole time he was gone reading books. The egg was still warm, intact, and spotless.

He looked at the egg for a long time, breathing deeply and thinking. It seemed as if he were completely lost in thought.

"I hadn't realized that of all your sisters, *you* would be the perfect woman, Robin."

I smiled demurely and cast my eyes to the side. "I didn't realize the measure of a perfect woman was the same as a broody hen."

"You'd be surprised how many people cannot keep one egg safe." He tucked the egg and keys in his pockets. "I'd like to announce our wedding date to the guests at the party."

"Sure." It wasn't like I was sticking around after that anyway.

WE HAD three weeks to come up with a plan. Lissy had found a cache of old clothing – presumably that of previous brides – during her time in the mansion. She gave me directions to it, and as furtively as I could, we scavenged together evening dresses that suited both of my sisters.

I ordered my masquerade costume online and refused to tell Fitcher what I was going to dress as. When it arrived, I hauled the huge box to my room without opening it.

While we were planning the party, Fitcher fussed and tutted about balancing getting the starlet to rub the right elbows while still announcing our wedding. He seemed weirdly excited to be marrying me. We were in the ballroom together with the florist when I noticed the balcony.

There was a small railing on the second floor above the wide double doors that led to the ballroom. A small pair of French doors were framed behind the balcony. It was perfect.

"I could stand up there." I pointed at the little curtained doors. "And you could make the announcement."

When Fitcher and the starlet looked at me, confused that I had any ideas at all about their party, I continued. "It keeps me out of the crowd, where she should be mingling. It makes me less of a distraction. But still... honored?" I tested out the theory.

Fitcher beamed.

The starlet nodded.

The last bit of my plan had fallen into place.

MY PLAN WAS COMPLICATED and precise. Each portion needed to occur in exactly the right order. I placed items I would need as the evening progressed in caches around the enormous house. A box here. A dress form there. Arsonist's gear in another place.

The first order of business was to get my sisters out of the house. Well after the party was begun, but just thirty minutes before I was to appear on the balcony for the big announcement, my sisters donned their party attire and masks. They were also dripping in the jewelry that Fitcher had showered each of us with. A king's ransom in gems.

In a gown and mask, myself, to blend in through the small crowd on the ground floor, we made our ways to the limousines parked in the circular driveway in front of the mansion.

As discussed, my sisters acted like they were drunk, and began loudly arguing with one another. I ushered them to Fitcher's own driver and poured them into the back of the limo. Briefly removing my mask, so the driver would know who I was, I commanded him to take them to their hotel. It was a small bed and breakfast two houses down the lane from our mother's house. Even in heels, they would be able to walk the rest of the way home.

I told him to not pause or look back, and the moment he dropped them off, to return, as we might need more of his services. The bartenders were pouring particularly heavy drinks.

Step one, complete.

I dashed to the second-floor balcony and arranged the dress form. Using what I'd hoped was a model of a human skull from Fitcher's study (and not the real thing), I dressed the mannequin in bright flowers and a wedding veil. The small timer attached to a spotlight was the final touch. Set for the moment that Fitcher planned to announce our betrothal.

Step two, complete.

Now, shimmying out of my formal gown and gilded mask, I unpacked the box that had been delivered days prior. The absurdity of donning a massive chicken costume almost caused me to giggle in anxiety. With my hands shaking and my guts threatening to liquefy, I managed to don what was essentially a mascot costume of a big pink bird.

Step three, complete.

I could hear the commotion of the announcement in the distant ballroom. But the arsonist's supplies were at the corner of the house nearest the bloody basement chamber. I wanted the fire to have a good hold on the house before it was discovered. And I wanted it to destroy enough of the house to lay bare that secret room.

I ran into Mrs. Murphy on my way to my last cache.

"I'm sorry dear, who are you, have you gotten lost?" she asked, pursing her lips.

I did a comical dance and waved my chicken tail feathers at her. "I'm Fitcher's bird – a big surprise for Robin. There's a big reveal after the announcement of the wedding. There are a few more of our dancing troupe. We are supposed to rush in from different directions."

She chuckled and nodded and waved for me to carry on.

The fire was set. The blaze would be contained for a little while in the rooms where I'd destroyed the sprinklers. But once it reached the study, the rest of the house would be alerted to the danger. As I made my way out the side door, I ran into the butler.

"I believe you've lost your way," he said, gravely. Again, I shook my tailfeathers.

"I'm Fitcher's bird – a big surprise for Robin. There's a big reveal after the announcement of the wedding. There are a few more of our dancing troupe. We are supposed to rush in from different directions."

He smiled and rolled his eyes and let me pass.

I had to get out of there immediately. The light on the balcony had come on, and from the oohs and ahs I could hear in the ballroom, the decoy was still temporarily working.

I sprinted out the side door and toward the dark woods. Fitcher's limo driver stopped me on the road. I had not yet removed the chicken head. But my fully costumed sprint had to look both bizarre and comedic to the driver.

"Hey there, you're going the wrong way, the party is that way." The limo driver called through the window.

I shook my tail feathers at him in complete absurdity. "I'm Fitcher's Bird," I told him. "Fitcher wants to entertain and celebrate with people as they drive out of the woods. I have to get to my place on time."

The driver had seen enough of Fitcher's parties to buy the lie. I did not feel guilty about sending him back to the burning house. He wouldn't be waiting inside.

I could smell the smoke through the mesh eye holes of the massive chicken head.

Step four was complete.

My phone vibrated in my pocket. A small electric car drove up. The driver looked baffled.

"Did you call for a rideshare?" He asked, looking at his phone.

"I did." I pulled the chicken head off and slid into the tiny backseat of the man's car. "Do a three point turn here, we're too far to turn around ahead." I advised.

By the time we got to my mother's house, and found my sisters waiting at the door, we were watching police cars flowing down the road to the woods. Only one firetruck had answered the call. But police car after police car ran their blue lights toward Fitcher's mansion.

The head of my chicken suit was stuffed with jewelry, gold and gemstones. Old Fitcher wouldn't need those things in jail, anyway.

21

THREE YEARS

By the time the eldest child could walk, and I was thick with the second child, the stories had stopped featuring duplicitous women and rich men.

By the time the second boy could walk, and the eldest was able to ask for stories himself, the stories featured generous men and faithful mystics among the djinn and the magic talismans.

And once the third boy was born, I was tired of begging for my life every night. I was tired of protecting my children from their father's murderous gaze. I was tired of telling stories.

He laughed when I said so.

"I decided a long time ago to let you live, Sharzâd. That we could build a life together." He drew me into his sweaty arms across the bed. "I thought you knew that."

I didn't want to build a life with him. He'd killed Mariam. He'd killed hundreds of women before her. By staying alive this long, I'd saved a thousand and one women.

He had no idea I'd been the one who programmed his guns.

AUTHOR'S NOTE

It took me several years to figure out how to retell a fairy tale. As writer of sci-fi, fantasy, and horror, the leap into fairy tales was a relatively smooth one. It came during my grad school work in a program of Mythological Studies and Depth Psychology, which helped me formulate my techniques and theory around the process.

The first fairy tale retelling I wrote was "Ramps and Rocket" for an anthology call. Retelling the Rapunzel narrative as a diesel punk story was interesting to me on several levels, not the the least of which was scholarly. "Ramps and Rocket," "Survival Protocols," and "A Bird for a Bird" were all based on Donald Kalsched's analyses in *The Inner World of Trauma*.

Many of the tales chosen for this collection are the favorites of mine that are not likely to find another home in magazines or anthologies. As I revisit them, I can see myself reflected in them - it is my hope that readers may, too, see themselves in the stories.

My ongoing adventures in writing are available at https://aliciakinganderson.com/

ABOUT THE ARTIST

Cover artist Katherine Bierman is an American interdisciplinary artist.

Born in New York, Bierman earned her BFA in Fiber, with a concentration in Sustainability and Social Practice from the Maryland Institute College of Art in Baltimore, Maryland in 2015. Since graduating Bierman has worked in a variety of creative capacities in commercial, non-profit, and government sectors, and her own independent practice.

Bierman's intricately detailed drawings highlight the simultaneous beauty and terror of life. Her work is born from her personal experiences of love, death, grief, and hope. It is rich in symbolism, drawing upon nature, mythos, folklore, and occulture to illustrate the subconscious and its struggles, yearnings and emotions. These fantastical visions grapple with, and materialize meaning from her own profound life shifts, bearing the weight of experience that language fails to express.

Her work can be found at www.katherinelynnbierman.com